Escape to

Love

Escape to

Love

Vanessa

Miller

Book 5
Praise Him Anyhow Series

Publisher's Note:

This short story is a work of fiction. References to real events, organizations, or places are used in a fictional context. Any resemblances to actual persons, living or dead are entirely coincidental.

Vanessa Miller
www.vanessamiller.com

Printed in the United States of America
© 2013 by Vanessa Miller

Praise Unlimited Enterprises
Charlotte, NC

Other Books by Vanessa Miller

How Sweet The Sound
Heirs of Rebellion
The Best of All
Better for Us
Her Good Thing
Long Time Coming
A Promise of Forever Love
A Love for Tomorrow
Yesterday's Promise
Forgotten
Forgiven
Forsaken
Rain for Christmas (Novella)
Through the Storm
Rain Storm
Latter Rain
Abundant Rain
Former Rain

Anthologies (Editor)
Keeping the Faith
Have A Little Faith
This Far by Faith

EBOOKS
Love Isn't Enough

A Mighty Love

The Blessed One (Blessed and Highly Favored series)

The Wild One (Blessed and Highly Favored Series)

The Preacher's Choice (Blessed and Highly Favored Series)

The Politician's Wife (Blessed and Highly Favored Series)

The Playboy's Redemption (Blessed and Highly Favored Series)

Tears Fall at Night (Praise Him Anyhow Series)

Joy Comes in the Morning (Praise Him Anyhow Series)

A Forever Kind of Love (Praise Him Anyhow Series)

Ramsey's Praise (Praise Him Anyhow Series)

Escape to Love (Praise Him Anyhow Series)

Praise For Christmas (Praise Him Anyhow Series)

His Love Walk (Praise Him Anyhow Series)

Prologue

"I won't do it, Marlin. I can't believe you're asking me to do something like this." A year ago, Renee Thomas thought she had met the love of her life, but day by day as other things got in their way, the love they had was steadily dwindling.

"It's not like you haven't done it before. Stop being a prude," Marlin Jones said.

"I can't even believe you're bringing that up. You put something in my drink. I know you did it, Marlin."

"I don't have time to argue with you." He shoved a drink in her face. "Swallow this and let's get this show on the road."

"I can't drink," she told him while touching her belly. "I'm pregnant."

"You're what?!" Marlin stepped back, fixing his mouth as if he'd swallowed something foul as he stared at her. "You can't be serious. You better tell me something quick, because this is not how I do business."

"What business? I thought you and I were in love. Don't people that are in love have children together?"

"You knew I didn't want kids when we got together."

"It's not as if I planned it."

"Whose kid is it?" Marlin demanded.

"What kind of question is that? I haven't cheated on you." Renee couldn't stand the sight of Marlin sometimes. He'd been like a prince to her the first few months, taking her on shopping trips, exotic vacations and moving her into his mansion. She thought he loved her and wanted to be with her forever. But things had changed.

"Don't give me that crap. We both know you've cheated on me."

"And we both know that you're a liar and a fraud. I have the paperwork to prove it, so don't mess with me."

He swung around, stood in front of the window and took a few deep breaths. When he turned back towards her, he put the drink in her face again. "I don't have time for this. Drink up and let's get to it."

She took the drink from him. But instead of swallowing it, she threw it in his face. "I hate you."

Snarling like a wild animal, Marlin lunged at her. Renee's eyes widened in fear as she tried to escape the blows he punished her body with. She cried out for help as he knocked her down in front of the fireplace and began kicking her. "Help me, he's trying to kill my baby. Please help!" she screamed at the top of her lungs, knowing that Marlin had guests downstairs. She prayed that someone would come to her rescue.

"No one's going to help you. Don't you get it? You belong to me and I can do whatever I want to you."

"I'm not a slave. You can't do this to me."

"Who are you to tell me what I can or can't do? You're nothing." He grabbed her face and pulled her close as he said, "Get it through your dumb, thick head. You're nothing but what I tell you to be."

"My daddy didn't raise no dummies and I'm not going to be treated like this." She reached out and dug her nails deep into the hand holding her face.

Marlin snatched his hand back. When he saw the blood dripping down his fingers, he grimaced. "Now I'm going to really mess you up."

Renee desperately scanned the room and caught sight of the poker in front of the fireplace; she started crawling towards it. She wasn't just going to mess Marlin up if she got hold of it, she intended to gut him.

But Marlin saw what she was headed for and grabbed it before she could get to it. He then whipped her with it like she was a runaway slave who'd been brought back home in chains.

With every punishing blow, Renee screamed as if he was killing her, because the pain was just that bad. She tried protecting her stomach, but Marlin had no mercy and was now punching and kicking her again.

She could barely speak from the pain, but with the strength she had left, she begged, "Please stop."

He grabbed hold of her hair and yanked. "Are you as dumb as I think you are?"

She didn't fight it this time, just nodded.

"Say it," he demanded with a slap to her face.

"I'm dumb."

"And you're nothing without me, right?"

"I'm nothing," she agreed.

He left her alone then as he walked out of the room, mumbling about how she would be useless to him that night.

She lay on the floor sliding in and out of consciousness. When she was finally able to move, she crawled over to her cell and called for an ambulance. She hadn't admitted that she'd been beaten. Instead she told them she'd had an accident, because she didn't ever want anyone to know how truly worthless she was.

One

Looking herself over in the full length mirror, Renee Thomas liked what she saw. She'd often been compared to Angela Bassett. When Renee first began hearing the comparison, she felt compelled to remind people that Angela Bassett was in her fifties and old enough to be her mother. But then Renee realized just how ageless Angela Bassett seemed to be. She might be in her fifties, but the woman could pass for a thirty-something. So whenever she heard the compliment these days, Renee simply smiled and accepted it.

Outer beauty had never been a problem for Renee, but her inner beauty had taken a beating because of her dealings with Marlin Jones. He had constantly made her feel as if she couldn't do anything without him. The night he beat her and made her lose their child, had caused her self-esteem to sink even lower.

Her father and stepmother had been praying for her and after months of doubting herself, Renee was finally ready to re-enter the workforce. Wearing a navy blue suit, she grabbed her purse and headed out of the house. She'd messed up her life by making so many wrong choices in the past, but this was a new day for her, a new beginning.

"Looking good there, Ms. Thomas," Carmella Marshall-Thomas said as Renee entered the kitchen.

"You're looking pretty good yourself, Mrs. Thomas."

Carmella handed her a glass of orange juice and a bagel with vegetable cream cheese. "I figured you'd want something light to get you going."

"You're always so thoughtful." Renee kissed Carmella's cheek. "I haven't always been as thoughtful where you're concerned, but you're good people. I still miss my mom, but I am so thankful that my father married you."

"You're always going to miss your mom, Renee. I still miss mine. But you were so young when your mom died... I just wish you could've had more time with her."

"Yeah, me, too. But que sera sera, right?"

"I used to believe that. Now I believe that what we pray for is what will be."

Renee didn't respond to that because she sure didn't believe it. Yeah sure, when her brother, Ram came up against some woman he couldn't handle because she was too crazy to be rational, the family had prayed, and even she had prayed for Ram. And yes, God delivered Ram out of that woman's hands. But Renee had been through too much in her life to believe that God just sat around heaven waiting to answer her prayers. If that was the case, her mother would still be alive and she wouldn't have miscarried her baby.

"I know you don't believe me. But just know that I'm praying for you anyway," Carmella told her.

Renee smiled. "Just make sure you center them prayers around me getting a job, and quick. I'm starting to feel like I'm Ronny."

"You leave Ronny alone; he is doing just fine. His company has really taken off. I wouldn't be surprised if he pulls in a million or more this year."

"In that case, I might just be asking my brother for a job, if this interview doesn't pan out."

"O ye of little faith," Carmella said as she kissed Renee's forehead. "Go get that job."

Renee got in her car and headed for her interview. She was meeting with an internet mogul who'd found instant success after starting a social media website that was like Facebook, but this particular site was strictly for professionals. No videos of cats or messages about a person's hum drum life... nothing but wheeling and dealing went on twenty-four hours a day. If a person had a business, they wanted to be on this site. Consequently, advertisers also flocked to the site.

The professional media site had grown so fast that Pro-Site was now going public and needed an assistant to help one of the co-owners get organized. If it wasn't so pathetic, Renee would laugh at how her life had turned out. She had an MBA, but was interviewing to get someone's coffee and run errands. It had been stupid to take a year and a half off from the job market.

But Renee thought she had finally kissed the right frog and would be living the princess lifestyle she'd always craved. After moving in with Marlin, Renee just knew that life would be filled with shopping, exotic vacations and love, lots of love. He'd allowed her to shop as much as she wanted on his Visa Signature, World Elite Master Card and his black American Express. The vacations to tropical islands were wonderful, as well. But Marlin didn't love anyone but himself and Renee found out the hard way that some fairytales could become your worst nightmare.

Even though she wished she was excelling in her career like the rest of her sisters and brothers, Renee wasn't going to cry over it. She was going to take her second chance by the horns and make the best of it.

As she parked her car, Renee received a text message. Thinking it was probably Carmella with some scripture for her to meditate on before going into her interview or a Praise alert, Renee pulled her phone out of her purse and read the message.

Tell your brother to stop harassing me or else.

The text was from Marlin. She had no idea what he was talking about, but Renee hoped that Ram wasn't involved in anything that had to do with Marlin. She quickly called her brother. When he picked up, she said, "I just received a text message from Marlin... something about you harassing him. What's that all about?"

"Ha!" Ram was practically giddy as he said, "He wishes I would take two seconds out of my day to think about an insect like him."

"Then what is he talking about?"

"I know he just applied for a loan at my bank and got turned down. Maybe he thinks it's my fault that his credit report indicates he's been taking out loans all over town."

"He's a jerk; I'm glad you didn't give him the loan."

"Wasn't me. Someone else had that pleasure. I refuse to do business with that clown. His money is no good with me."

"Trust me, brother, Marlin's money is no good in more ways than you know."

"Don't respond to him. He just wants to have something to say to you."

"I'm deleting his message the moment I hang up with you. Don't worry. I want nothing to do with Marlin Jones, or anyone like him, for that matter."

"Good."

"Talk to you later. I'm on my way into a job interview." They hung up and she deleted Marlin's text just as she said. She then turned off her phone and got ready for her new beginning.

***

Jason Morris was seated in the conference room with his executive staff planning out the strategy for the most important IPO of his life. If all went well, the company would be worth billions and he and his business partner would be able to walk away multi-millionaires. If things went really well, they would join the billionaire's club.

"Now I don't have to explain to anyone in this room the necessity for closed lips. Nothing we discuss is to be repeated outside of these walls."

Heads nodded around the room.

"These next few months will make or break us. So I'm going to need dedication and long nights... if you have vacation plans, scrap 'em. If we keep our heads down and work hard this next month, I promise you, it will feel like Christmas every day around here after we finalize this public offering. Now are you with me?"

"Of course," Larry, his right hand man said. "I'm in it to win it. So if I have to cancel a few dates for a while, I'm sure I'll survive."

One of the women said, "I have kids, so I may have to take work home from time to time, but I'm in as well."

"Thanks, Sally, I appreciate your dedication. I know how important your children are to you and I promise I won't make you sacrifice your time with them for too long."

She nodded.

"Well," Jason clasped his hands together. "Let's get to work."

His team scattered and then Jason went to his office and grabbed his coffee cup. He was in for a long day and needed to fill up on the blackest coffee he could find. He went into the break room and poured the coffee in his cup, took a couple of sips and then headed back down the hall towards his office.

Jason caught sight of a beautiful woman standing in front of his secretary's desk. He rubbed his eyes, figuring that fatigue had already set in, then glanced at her again. That's when he realized that his eyes weren't playing tricks on him. Renee Thomas, the girl he'd attended high school with and youth group at church... she was also the same girl he'd carried a secret crush on for more years than he could count. He hadn't seen her since high school. Now she was standing about five feet in front of him and suddenly he became that shy, gangly kid again.

He'd almost worked up the nerve to ask Renee out during tenth grade biology class, only to discover that Renee had started dating his best friend. So Jason contented himself with playing the field and quietly pining after the one woman he couldn't have. Then after graduation they all went off to college. Now they were all grown up.

Unbuttoning his jacket, Jason puffed out his chest as he walked toward her. He now had muscles, biceps and certainly wasn't shy around the ladies anymore. He was determined not to be shaken and to remember who he was now. "Renee Thomas, what on earth are you doing here?"

She turned toward him. It took a moment, but recognition shone through her eyes as she said, "Oh my God, I didn't know you still lived in Raleigh." She wrapped her arms around him and hugged him tight.

"I moved back last year," he told her as they ended the embrace.

"I'm glad to know that you still live here."

"I actually just moved back a few months ago. I was living in Charlotte... my brothers live there."

"Ramsey and Ronny are in Charlotte?"

"Yeah, and I have another brother through marriage now. His name is Dontae. He lives there also."

"Your dad re-married?" Renee nodded and then Jason said, "Good for him. He deserves some happiness." There was a brief moment of silence and then Jason asked, "So what brings you to our little company today?"

"I have an interview with Mr. Richards, but I think he must have forgotten about my appointment, because he's not here."

Jason's secretary chimed in. "You know how Dean gets when he's programing."

Jason turned back to Renee and said, "I apologize for my business partner. But if memory serves, he was supposed to be interviewing for an assistant this week. I've been on him to get someone to help get him organized, and believe me, he really needs the help."

"That's good because I really need the job. If earning my MBA taught me nothing else, I've certainly learned a few organizational techniques that I could use to help Mr. Richards."

Jason wondered why someone with Renee's credentials would be interviewing for an entry level position. She should have years of experience by now, but he didn't want to pry, so he turned to Dawn and asked, "Can you give Renee a tour of the office and then put her to work at getting Dean organized?"

"But what if Mr. Richards doesn't want to hire me?" Renee asked.

"You worry about getting Dean organized and let me worry about getting you hired," Jason told her as he walked away, thinking that he didn't need his coffee to get him going any more. His mind would be running a mile a minute with thoughts of Renee Thomas.

Two

"I got the job!" Renee screamed as she came through the front door.

Carmella was in the kitchen finishing her dinner preparations. She wiped her hands with the dry towel and rushed to meet up with Renee. They grabbed hands and jumped up and down. "You got it... you really got it."

"I couldn't believe it. But I kept telling myself that today was my new beginning and look what happened."

"Look what God *made* happen."

Renee stopped jumping. She walked into the kitchen shaking her head. Carmella followed and when they sat down behind the counter, Renee said, "I'm not sure you can credit God with this one. An old friend of mine from high school is one of the partners in the company. I hadn't seen him in years, but the guy I was supposed to interview with today wasn't there, so Jay said that I could just have the job. I didn't even interview for it."

All of that sounded like the favor of God to Carmella, but Renee just didn't get it. Carmella wasn't interested in beating anyone over the head with the knowledge of Christ, so she simply said, "I'm so happy for you, Renee." She pointed toward the stove. "Fix yourself some dinner. I need to go upstairs and take care of something."

With a heavy heart Carmella climbed the stairs and went to her throne room. It actually used to be Dontae's bedroom, but ever since he moved out, Carmella had been using the room as part office, part prayer room. She worried about Renee sometimes. The things she'd been through in her young life had caused her to doubt God. Carmella decided that it was time for her to stop worrying and start praying.

Opening the door she stepped into her throne room and then fell on her knees and steepled her hands as she lowered her head. "Lord God, I thank You for all that You've done for my family. You've kept us safe from seen and unseen dangers and I'm grateful for Your faithfulness. I know that it is in You that we live, move and have our being, but Renee doesn't know that. She doesn't believe that she can trust You with her life, so I'm asking that You make it plain for her. Show Renee that You are not just my God, but hers as well. Bring her closer to You and join her in relationship with Your son, Jesus Christ.

"I thank you in advance for everything You are about to do for Renee, believing that You will perform Your word in her life. I believe it because You've already shown me through Joy, Dontae and Ramsey that You are well able to bring them to the knowledge of God better than I could ever dream of. I don't know how You are going to work things out, but I trust You. So, I'm calling on my Lord

Jesus and a multitude of angels to bring Renee into the kingdom. Amen, in Jesus' matchless name I pray unto You."

When she finished praying, she went back downstairs and found her husband and Renee at the kitchen table eating the roast she'd made for dinner. She kissed Ramsey. "I didn't know you were home."

"I just got here. I've been listening to Renee. Did she tell you about her new job?"

"Sure did." Carmella fixed her plate and then sat down with her family. She said grace over her food and then asked Renee, "Do you start tomorrow, or do you have to wait until they do a background check?"

"Jay really got me the hook up. I'm in, no waiting on drug or background checks. They put me to work today, so I have to go back bright and early tomorrow."

"You sound excited, sweetie," Ramsey observed.

Wiping her mouth with a napkin, Renee said, "I am, Daddy. I mean, earlier this morning I was feeling down about the time I've wasted, and about the fact that I was applying for an assistant position when I should be at manager or director level by now. But then I ran into Jay." She hunched her shoulders. "And I don't know... I guess it just didn't matter anymore."

Ramsey turned to Carmella and said, "Jay and Renee were in youth group at our old church when she was a kid."

"Oh, I didn't know that. Renee only mentioned that they attended high school together." Carmella turned toward Renee.

With a look of *guilty* written on her face, Renee admitted, "I knew if I mentioned church, you'd swear that God was up to something. And I guess I just didn't want to hear it."

Mmm, Carmella thought, sounds like she needed to go back to the throne room and pray about this guy named Jay.

***

The next morning, Renee finally met her elusive boss, Dean Richards. The man fascinated her. Because he looked anything but the picture of success that Jay projected. Dean's movements were awkward. His bifocal glasses didn't seem to help him find blue prints and drafts that were on his messy desk. He was as unkempt as he was disorganized. The man was a genius who looked as if he needed directions to his own home. She understood why Jay was so desperate to get help for his business partner. Dawn informed her that Jay was nervous about Dean's disorganization because a lot of paperwork needed for the IPO was missing. When she applied for this position, Renee didn't have any hopes of being able to put that MBA her father paid for to good use. But now that she knew an IPO was at stake, she worked diligently, gathering all of the paperwork from Dean's office.

The man had things piled in stacks or just thrown in a corner, in boxes or all over his desk. It would take her at least a week to get things to the point where she could start creating files for the documents and inputting the information into the computer. She wasn't discouraged, though, Renee was filled with a determination to do the best job she could. Jay was counting on her and she wasn't going to let him down.

By the time Renee felt that she had a handle on her work, it was one in the afternoon and her stomach was growling. Dawn sat at the desk across from her. She must have heard her empty stomach because she said, "The graphics department ordered a bunch of pizzas for lunch. There's still a couple of boxes in the break room if you're hungry."

"Thanks, I am getting hungry." Renee went into the break room, grabbed a paper plate and opened one of the pizza boxes. Pepperoni and sausage was in the first box. Renee was hungry, but not hungry enough to eat meat on her pizza. She opened the next box and then the next. Finally she found the box that held the cheese-only pizza. She took a slice and put it in the microwave.

"Don't tell me that you still don't like pepperoni pizza," Jason said.

She swung around and saw that he was leaning against the wall. "How long have you been there?"

"Long enough to see you rummage through every pizza box in the break room. I'm glad you finally found a slice to your liking."

She pulled her pizza out of the microwave and took a bite. "The best pizza is the simplest." Turning toward Jason she asked, "And how did you remember that, anyway?"

He was still leaning against the wall, studying her as if she were a Picasso. "I remember a lot about you."

Moving away from the wall to stand closer to Renee he added, "Like the fact that you and Rob Dukes were madly in love."

Smirking, Renee said, "Rob was madly in love with a lot of women. He broke up with me the first week of college. Said he needed to explore his options."

Jason's nostrils flared. Shaking his head, he told her, "I wish I had known that he'd done that to you. I would have taken care of him for you."

Renee laughed. "I wouldn't have asked you to do that."

Jason leaned back and looked into her eyes. "You don't think I could have taken him, do you?"

Still laughing, Renee said, "I didn't say that. But you were a basketball player, you practiced dribbling in your free time. Rob was a football player and a wrestler, he swung people around and knocked them down for fun. And he had about fifty pounds on you."

"Okay, maybe I wouldn't have been able to take him back then. But I've got a few muscles now." He flexed in front of her. "I might just go find him now and teach him a lesson about leaving a beautiful woman to nurse her broken heart. You probably received terrible grades that first semester, right? Somebody has to pay for that."

She shook her head. "Straight A's my first and second semester. So, Rob didn't cause much heartache, after all. He was all wrong for me." She shrugged. "And believe me, I have a long history of picking the wrong guys."

"I don't like the sound of that. I always thought you deserved the very best. I knew that Rob wasn't the right guy for you, but I didn't know how to tell you."

Trying to keep the mood light, Renee told him, "You were too busy dating every available girl in sight to worry about me."

"Not fair. I only dated those girls because the one girl I wanted wasn't available. She was too busy wasting her time with a meat head."

Renee took a bite of her pizza and stepped away from the fire. Every inch of Jason Morris was divine. He was a chocolate coated pretty boy with hazel eyes that seemed to draw her in. And that captivating smile of his was killer. However, Marlin had been handsome and pleasing to her eyes, as well. Her brother had once told her that in a room full of good, she had a knack for finding bad. But this was a new day and she wasn't falling and bumping her head so quickly this time. "I'd better get back to work."

Renee spent the next hour working with Dawn to get a handle on the telephone system. Dawn had an afternoon appointment, so she needed Renee to take messages for both Dean and Jason who would be in meetings the rest of the afternoon.

By 4 o'clock Renee had taken several business calls for both Dean and Jason, but she had also taken calls from Marlene and Nina for Jason. Both of those calls sounded very personal and left Renee feeling as if she'd made the right decision in backing away from Jason in the break room.

Jason's phone rang again. "Pro-Site, Jason Morris' office, may I help you?"

"Yes, is Jay in? This is Tiffany."

Why was this woman calling him Jay? Everyone always called him Jason. Renee had been the one to shorten his name to Jay when they were in youth group. "Mr. Morris is in a meeting. Can I take a message?"

"Yes, please tell him that I cleared my calendar, so I'll be able to make our date tomorrow night after all."

Yep, Renee thought as she hung up the phone, you made the right decision this time, girl... Just keep dodging those bullets. She finished up her work and tried to put Jason, the playboy, and all of his women out of her mind. By the time she packed up and left work for the day, Renee was feeling good about all that she had been able to accomplish. Jason would be happy to know that Dean was well on his way to being the picture of organization.

But as she stepped outside and saw Marlin leaning against the bumper of her car, a chill went through her so deep that it caused her bones to ache. She started to run back into the building, but then Marlin yelled. "I'm not going to leave until we talk."

She knew it was true; he'd hang out there all night just to get under her skin. Marching over to her car she said, "Why can't you just leave me alone?"

Marlin got in her face. "Nothing but death will ever part us. You belong to me, and I don't let go of what's mine so easily."

"Have you lost your mind? After everything you did to me, do you honestly think I'd be stupid enough to come back to you?"

Confusion shaped his brows. "I don't think that would be stupid at all. We were good together." Marlin reached out and touched a strand of Renee's hair. "You're the one for me and I'm the one for you."

Renee smacked his hand away. "Yeah, I used to feel that way... right up until the time you beat my baby out of me."

"That was an accident, and you know it. You've done things to me, too, Renee. But I'm not throwing any of it in your face. I have forgiven you."

"Mighty generous of you, especially since I never did anything to you. But if you're waiting on some forgiveness from me, it will be a long time coming."

"You're talking crazy. You started that fight when you threw that drink in my face."

He couldn't even look her in the face as he told that lie. From the moment she told him she was pregnant, he'd wanted to beat her. She saw it in his eyes that night. Evidently being pregnant spoiled all his plans for her. "Just stay away from me. Go back to Charlotte and find someone else to treat like dirt."

She attempted to walk away from him and he grabbed hold of her arm, yanking her back. "Don't you walk away from me."

She'd heard the same snarl in his voice the night he attacked her. The last thing she wanted was for her new co-workers to see her being attacked. So she tried to defuse the situation by saying, "Calm down, Marlin, we're in a public place. You don't want to go to jail, do you?"

"Stop acting stupid and there won't be a reason for me to go to jail." Pulling her towards his car, he said, "You're coming with me."

"No... no!"

"What's going on out here?" Jason said as he approached them in the parking lot.

"Mind your business; this doesn't concern you," Marlin said as he tried to open his passenger door.

"He's trying to kidnap me. Help!" Renee screamed.

Jason reached them in one second flat. He grabbed hold of Renee and pulled her away from Marlin, while shoving her behind him. "I suggest you get out of here before I call the police and report this incident."

"You shouldn't put your nose where it doesn't belong," Marlin said as he jumped in his car. As he was leaving he rolled the window down and yelled, "This isn't over."

"It's been over," Renee yelled back and then fell into Jason's arm as the tears rolled down her cheeks. What was wrong with her? How could she have ever fallen for someone as abusive as Marlin? Her brother tried to warn her about him, but she hadn't listened and now she couldn't get rid of him.

"I'm calling the police. You need to file a report."

"No, please. I don't want to get the police involved."

"Who is that guy? Why don't you want to call the police on him?"

"He's just an ex-boyfriend who doesn't want to put a period on it and move on. But I'll take care of it. I'll make sure he knows that he can't come to my job."

"He looked pretty aggressive to me. And you were terrified. I could see it all over your face."

Walking back toward her car, she said, "I'm fine. It's no big deal."

He reached out and grabbed her arm, Renee flinched as if she thought he was about to hit her. Jay released her arm and slowly stepped back. Jay stared at her for a moment. As his eyes filled with knowledge, he said, "You need to file a restraining order against him. No man has the right to put his hands on a woman."

What kind of fool was she? Why hadn't she taken out a restraining order against Marlin already? But even as she chastised herself for being so foolish, she knew the reason. It was the same reason she didn't want the police called now. She had been ashamed of what Marlin had done to her and thought that taking out the restraining order might alert her family to everything she'd been through. She took a deep breath, realizing that it was time to stop hiding and start fighting back.

Glancing at her watch, she said, "You're right. I should have done that a long time ago. The courthouse is closed by now. But if Mr. Richards won't mind, I can file it first thing in the morning."

"He won't mind. I'll make sure of it."

"Thanks, Jay." They stood there for a moment staring into each other's eyes again. Renee began wondering if Jay was, in fact, one of the good guys or just another bad boy in disguise. "Well, I guess I'll head home now."

But instead of going home, Renee drove to Carmella's bakery. On Tuesdays her stepmother normally stayed late doing bookkeeping and handling any other details that needed her attention. If she was going to finally put that restraining order out on Marlin, then she needed to confide in someone about what happened to her while she was with him. Renee trusted Carmella and knew that anything she shared with her would stay between them.

"Hey, what brings you by the store today?" Carmella asked as Renee walked in.

"I was hoping that you could spare a few minutes for me."

Carmella was in the middle of wiping down the tables. She put the towel back in the bucket and said, "Of course I have time. Sit down and let's talk."

"Do you mind if we talk in your office?"

Carmella gave her a look that said she'd been waiting for this moment. "Come on," she said as Renee followed her to the back.

"Sit down, hon. Do you want me to call your father? Or is this conversation strictly between us?"

Even though her heart was heavy, Renee smiled. Carmella never let her down. "I just want to talk to you. I don't think I could handle telling Daddy any of this."

"I thought things were going well for you. But you look so hurt and lost right now that I'm getting a little worried about what you have to say."

Sitting across from Carmella, Renee began, "Do you remember how I told everyone that I had been bullied in middle school?"

"Yes, I remember that. It was the same day we found out what happened with Dontae and his coach."

"Well, I feel like I'm being bullied again." Tears cascaded down her face as she detailed the nightmare she had experienced with Marlin. "I never admitted it, but you all know that Marlin beat me and caused me to lose our baby."

Carmella nodded.

The tears kept coming as Renee said, "What I've tried to keep from you and Daddy was the reason it happened. But I can't keep hiding."

Carmella was crying with her. She wiped away the tears on Renee's face. "You don't have to tell me anything. I can see how hurt you are over this."

Renee vehemently shook her head. "It's gone too far. I need to file a restraining order against Marlin. The only reason I haven't done it yet, is because I've been so afraid that he might tell all of you what he did to me. And I never wanted anyone to know." Carmella handed her some tissue. Renee blew her nose and then continued. "Marlin wanted me to sleep with one of his business associates."

"My dear Lord, I had no clue that Marlin was so evil."

"He's worse than that. He once spiked my drink and then let another one of his business associates sleep with me. I don't remember doing anything with the guy, but I woke up in bed with him. The reason he beat me that night was because I refused a drink he tried to serve me. He had another man waiting downstairs that he wanted me to entertain."

"That's just sick. What in the world would make Marlin think that kind of behavior is okay?"

"He's the very spawn of Satan, if you ask me," Renee said as she wiped her tears away. "He tricked me into believing he was a loving, kind and generous man, when all the while he was nothing like that. Anything I got from Marlin, I paid dearly for it."

"In my day, if a man passed you off to one of his friends that was a clear sign that he didn't want you anymore. But you're telling me that he hasn't stopped harassing you."

"He thinks he owns me or something. But I'll never go back to him. I would kill him first."

"Let's hope it doesn't come to that. Now, I'll go with you to the courthouse in the morning so that we can put out a restraining order against him."

"Please don't tell Daddy. I know I'm asking a lot because the two of you don't keep secrets from each other. But I can't bear for him to know what happened to me."

"That is a tough one. What I can promise you is that I will step aside and give you the time needed to talk to your father about this. But I think you will find that your father is more understanding than you know."

***

At that moment Ramsey was standing just outside Carmella's office. And he was anything but understanding. A rage was building in him that he'd never known before. Someone had hurt his child in the most vile way possible. If he got his hands on Marlin Jones, Renee wouldn't have to worry about a restraining order, that's for sure.

"Lord Jesus, help me. I don't know if I can turn this one over to You."

Then Ramsey thought of how his son, Ramsey Jr. had almost lost his life because he tried to handle matters himself instead of turning them over to the Lord. But even with that knowledge fresh in his memory, Ramsey couldn't stop himself from plotting his next move.

Three

After three weeks on the job, Renee had finally gotten Dean's office in order. But there were a few things that she hadn't been able to make sense of. Two items that she found could possibly hurt the upcoming public offering, so she left Dean a note, asking if he had time to discuss them. So far he had not made time to talk about the matter with her.

She spent the day working on Dean's expense reports, hoping that he would finish his programing soon so they could have their meeting.

Her cell phone rang. Renee didn't recognize the number; curiosity got the best of her and she answered the call.

"That restraining order isn't worth the paper it's written on," Marlin yelled through the phone.

She glanced at her caller ID again. The number that showed up was not Marlin's. She didn't know if he had borrowed someone else's phone just so he could harass her, or if he had gotten a new phone after she blocked his number, but she wasn't going to entertain him for one second. She hit the end button on her cell and got back to work.

"If Dean sees you answering your cell during work hours, he's going to have a fit. His head is in the clouds most of the time, but he seems to have a radar for cell phones," Dawn reminded her.

"It won't happen again." Renee turned her cell off.

"You know I got your back, girl. Next time you get an important call, just head to the break room or take the call to the bathroom."

"Renee," Dean hollered from his office, as he normally did when his office door was open and he needed her. But Renee wasn't complaining. She was enjoying her job.

"Must be his radar," Dawn said.

"I hope not. I actually like this job." Renee got up and went into Dean's office. As usual, he looked unkempt and out of sorts. "Did you sleep here again last night?"

"Got to... we're about to take my new program live and I have to get all the bugs out of it beforehand or the IPO that Jason is working on will blow up in all of our faces."

"You're a busy man, I get it. But you still have to make time for yourself. You won't be any good to Jay or your family," *Did he even have a family?* "if you crash and burn."

He waved a hand in the air. "Yeah, yeah, I know. All work, no play and all of that. But don't cry for me. I have plans for a weekend full of nothing but fun and sun."

"Good," she said, she then became uneasy as Dean stared at her as if he wanted her to join him on his fun/sun weekend. It was an odd look on Dean, because she'd never pictured him as a Neil Patrick Harris from How I Met Your Mother type, Dean was more like Jason Segel, the stable, dependable friend. "So, what did you call me in here for?"

"Oh yeah, back to business." He clasped his hands and stood up. "I can't find the developer file."

Renee smiled and went to the file cabinet she purchased for his office. She opened the third drawer down and pulled out the file he was looking for. "Do you need anything else?"

"You put a lot of my files on the computer, right?"

"Yes sir, I thought you'd be able to keep up with the documents you needed if they were just a click away."

"That was smart thinking. But I can't find any of the documents on my computer. Can you show me where they are?"

Renee smiled. Dean was a computer geek. He was good at programing web pages and working with graphics on the computer, but he couldn't find a simple Pages document. She thought that was funny. "You didn't have Pages installed on your computer, so I installed it so I would have a place to put your documents." Stepping behind his desk, she pointed at his computer. "She that little blue jar with the pen across it?"

He nodded.

"Click on it." When he did, Renee then showed him how to access his files. She stepped back around the desk.

"I don't know how I ever got along without you. Thanks for all the time and energy you expended to get me organized."

"You're welcome. Did you get a chance to look at the documents I had questions on?"

"My head is so jumbled with this new program that I can't wrap my brain around anything else right now."

"Those documents seem important. Would you rather that I discuss them with Jay?"

"I don't need you running to Jay behind my back. I'll review the documents when I get a chance."

"O-*kay*." She turned and started walking out of his office.

Before she reached the door, Dean said, "Sorry for snapping. I'm just really busy right now."

She swung back around. "I understand, don't worry about it."

He leaned back in his seat, stared at her a moment and then asked, "What are you doing this weekend?"

"Excuse me?"

"The executive staff has scheduled a retreat to the Bahamas to celebrate the release of Pro-Site 2. I think you should join us."

She knew about the retreat, but figured that she hadn't made enough of a contribution to accompany them on the trip, since she'd only been on the job for a few weeks. "Thanks for offering, but with such short notice, I don't think I could swing it."

"Well, think about. You could share a hotel room with Dawn."

"I don't get it. Why are you offering this trip to me? I haven't done anything but organize your paperwork. I haven't contributed enough to earn a trip to the Bahamas."

"That's what *you* think. If you hadn't gotten me organized, I wouldn't have been able to bring the programing in on time."

"Thanks for noticing the work I've done." She hesitated, then said, "Let me think about it. I'll let you know." Walking out of the room, Renee was still trying to figure out what had just happened. At first she thought Dean was coming on to her, but since he said she could share a room with Dawn, she figured that she might be wrong and this was just his way of showing appreciation for the work she'd done.

As she got back to work, the phone on her desk rang. She picked it up and Marlin was screaming, "You don't get to leave me; do you hear me... it's never going to be over between us."

"How did you get this number?"

"I know everything about you. You can't hide from me. Do I need to move to Raleigh to prove to you that I'm serious about us getting us back together?"

"That will never happen." She slammed down the phone.

Her phone started ringing again. Renee put her head in the palms of her hands. Frustration was setting in. She'd gotten the restraining order, he received it, but Marlin wouldn't quit. He wasn't going to leave her alone.

"You want me to get that?" Dawn asked.

"Please."

Dawn answered. She held the phone for a moment, listening and then said, "This is not Renee, but if you call here talking like that again, I will call the police and report you. Got that?"

"What did he say?" Renee asked.

"He said that if you hang up on him again, he's going to break your neck."

Blowing out a frustrated sigh, Renee confessed, "I don't know what to do."

"Call the police. Report him for harassment."

"I already have a restraining order against him. You see what he thinks of that."

Shaking her head, Dawn told her, "This is why the only men I date are saved for real, and they love Jesus more than me. So, if we break up, I just tell them to go pray about it, and ask the Lord to find that perfect woman he has designed for them."

"That's a good way to say buzz off. But Marlin wouldn't bite. I'm convinced he's the devil, so he's not hardly getting ready to pray about nothing."

"It sounds like you really got one. I'll be praying for you," Dawn offered.

With all these people praying for her, Renee wondered why her life kept going from bad to worse.

***

Coming upon Renee's desk, Jason heard the one-sided argument and knew who was on the other end of the phone. But what he couldn't figure out was how Renee could have gotten herself involved with someone like the man he saw her with a few weeks ago. In high school Renee had always seemed so confident, so vibrant. Everyone wanted to know her and be a part of her inner circle.

He'd once witnessed a man dragging a woman by her hair into oncoming traffic. Jason and a few other bystanders had jumped out of their cars and pulled the man off her. The man told all of them to back off and then barked at his woman to "Come on and get in the car."

But even knowing that she had been rescued and could go on her merry way, Jason had been amazed as he watched the woman's shoulders go slack as she kept her head down and followed her abuser to his car. That, to him, had been the picture of insecurity... a woman who thought she was nothing without a man. Whether that man was good for her or not didn't matter, she just needed a man to help her feel worthy of the life God had given her.

He would have never associated Renee with abuse. But as sure as he knew his name, he knew that Renee had been victimized at the hands of the man he saw her with a few weeks ago. He saw the fear in her eyes as he tried to pull Renee to his car. But more than that, he saw the sense of entitlement on Marlin's face... like he thought he owned a piece of Renee's soul.

Jason was now feeling a burden for Renee, like the one he'd felt the day he got out of his car to help a woman whose name he didn't even know. But the problem with that was, he also had a duty to the employees at his and Dean's company. So after work he met up with Renee in the parking lot. Standing by her car, he put his hand on her arm as he said, "I was wondering if I could take you to dinner so we could discuss something."

Renee shook her head, "I wouldn't want to keep you away from Tiffany."

"What about Tiffany?"

Smirking, Renee said, "Tiffany called and confirmed your movie date tonight."

"Well yeah, there's a movie she wants to see. But I have time for a quick dinner, because we need to talk about some things." Jason noticed that Renee's eyes rolled every time she mentioned Tiffany's name. Was she jealous?

"I already have dinner plans for this evening, so just tell me what you want me to know now, please."

"You seem angry. Have I done something to you?"

"I'm not angry." Renee took her car keys out of her purse. "I just don't have time for dates with men who already seem to have enough women to take on a date every day of the week."

Feeling as if his character was being assassinated, Jason put up his own wall of defense. "I wasn't asking you on a date. I simply wanted to talk with you about the harassing phone calls you've been getting at work. I have a duty to protect the other employees of this company, so you need to find a way to make this stop or we're going to have to make other arrangements."

Her mouth fell open as the shock of possibly losing her job set in. "You're firing me?"

"No, I'm not firing you. I'm going to hire a couple of security guards for our lobby area. My hope is that we'll deter him from coming on our property. But you need to make this stop, okay?"

Renee shook her head. "I promise. And I'm so sorry for bringing my problems to work. But if you'll give me a chance I will get this resolved. I really need this job; I can't afford to get fired."

It was almost as if her shoulders sagged right in front of him as he caught a glimpse of the insecurity he hadn't identified with Renee until now. Something had happened to her. He didn't know why it mattered to him, but a strong desire to help, swept over Jason. No matter what it cost him, he had to get to the bottom of the matter, and help restore Renee's confidence.

Four

Renee was meeting her father for dinner. He'd called and said he needed to talk to her. Right after hanging up with him, she'd called Carmella and asked, "Did you tell Dad anything?"

"About what you and I talked about?"

"Yeah."

"No, I've been praying about it, and waiting on you to tell him yourself."

Sighing with relief, Renee said, "Thanks. He invited me to dinner tonight and I got a little scared."

Now on her way to meet with her dad, Renee was reeling from the confrontation with Jason. She actually thought he was asking her out. Why on earth would a man like Jason want anything to do with someone like her? She was all messed up as if she'd come from a dysfunctional Kardashian-like family.

She got out of her car and began walking towards her dad's favorite Mexican restaurant as she hummed the tune to Kirk Franklin's Brighter Day. Her stepmother loved that song, but right now, Renee was only singing it in hopes of grabbing hold of the lyrics and making them a reality in her life.

But then she heard Marlin's voice as he came up behind her. "Who are you meeting here, that lover boy from work?"

Renee swung around and faced her enemy. "Leave me alone. Do you hear me? I don't owe you any explanations."

"Why did you let him touch you?"

"Who? What are you talking about?"

"I saw him touch your arm in the parking lot. That does not happen unless I give permission."

Her lip curled as she looked at the monster standing before her. He had left her with this unclean feeling and no matter how many times she tried to scrub it off, it remained. She opened her purse and started searching through it.

"What are you looking for? That little piece of paper the courts gave you?" He laughed in her face.

Renee felt powerless, and she was tired of feeling that way. She put her hands on the pepper spray she'd purchased a few days ago.

Marlin said, "What are you going to do... throw the paper at me?"

She was just about to blast him when she heard her father yelling, "Get away from my daughter." Ramsey rushed over to them, grabbed Marlin by the collar and pushed him against the building. "Stay away from her. Do you hear me? Or I swear before God that I will kill you the next time I catch you within fifty feet of her."

"Let him go, Dad. He's not worth it."

Ramsey jabbed his elbow up against Marlin's throat. "You like to harass women... like to treat them as if they're nothing but a pet to be ordered about in any way you see fit?"

Renee pulled at her father's arm. "Please, Dad. Don't do this."

Ramsey released the pressure of his elbow against Marlin's neck as he backed away and said, "It ends today. Right here and now, or I will deal with you."

Rubbing his neck, Marlin coughed a few times, trying to regain his voice and then said, "Are you threatening me?"

"No, I'm stating a fact and making you a promise." Ramsey took hold of Renee's arm. "Don't you ever come near my family again." With that they walked into the restaurant, leaving Marlin on the outside looking in.

"Carmella told you, didn't she?" Renee asked as she and her father were seated.

"No, Carmella kept her promise to you. Which is something I intend to speak with her about."

"How did you find out, then?"

"I was on my way into her office when I heard the two of you talking about what Marlin did to you. I knew that if I opened that door, you would clam up and I'd never get the full story out of you. So I just stood there and listened. But I never imagined that Carmella would be able to hold something like this from me for all these weeks."

"Don't be mad at her, Daddy. She knew that I couldn't bear it if you knew what had happened to me. I've been so ashamed of what I did."

Ramsey put a hand over his daughter's hand. "There's nothing for you to be ashamed of. That snake slipped something in your drink. You had no idea what you were doing."

"Yes, but Ram tried to warn me about Marlin. I wouldn't listen because I was intrigued by his money and power."

"Do you remember what I used to tell all of you kids when you were teenagers?"

Renee shook her head. "You've told us so much, I doubt I'd know what you're referring to."

"Sometimes, you just weren't listening." He patted her hand, gently admonishing her. "I told you that sin is never polite. It won't just take you so far and then ask, "Pretty please, can I take you a little farther? Once you open the door to sin, it will drag you as far away from God as it can take you."

Nodding Renee added, "And once sin has had its way, I'll be left to bear the guilt and shame of everything I did," she finished up one of the infamous lectures he'd passed on to each of them. "You were right, Dad. I've been so ashamed and filled with guilt that I let myself become a victim, rather than reach out to anyone in my family for help."

"Well, you're home now. And your family is here for you."

Before Renee could respond, two police officers rushed over to their table. "Ramsey Thomas?" the taller one asked.

"That's me," Ramsey said. "Can I help you?"

"Can you stand up, sir?"

Ramsey did what he was told. The other officer said, "Turn around and put your hands behind your back."

"What's going on?" Renee stood as if she could protect her father from the big bad policemen.

"Step back, ma'am. He's being arrested for battery."

"I didn't batter that little twerp. I should have, but I didn't."

"I have a restraining order against Marlin. He wasn't supposed to be anywhere near me. Why aren't you arresting him instead of my father?"

"We saw the marks on his neck so we have to take you in."

"He is stalking me. Don't you care about that?" Renee was screaming. The injustice of it all was making her want to tell these cops off and then hold out her wrist so they could cuff her, too.

"Hey, we're just doing our job. So step back," the police officer demanded.

Ramsey turned to Renee and said, "Do what they say. Just go call Carmella; tell her that I need to be bailed out of jail."

"This is a nightmare, and it's all my fault," Renee said, following the officers as they escorted her father to the police car.

Ramsey got in the backseat of the police car and said, "Stop blaming yourself, Renee and call Carmella for me."

"Okay, you're right. I'll meet you at the police station." She ran to her car, locked the doors and then called Carmella. "He's been arrested," Renee shouted as soon as Carmella picked up the phone.

"Who's been arrested?"

"Daddy. He wants you to meet him at the police station to bail him out." Then she quickly said, "I'll pay you and Daddy back. Whatever the cost, I'll pay it back," Renee promised.

"What happened?"

"Marlin followed me to the restaurant. Daddy saw him and went ballistic. Oh and just so you know, Daddy heard us talking that day I came to your office. And I can tell that he's upset with you for keeping my secret."

"Thanks for letting me know. I'll meet you at the police station."

***

Carmella paid the bond, but they still waited two hours before Ramsey was released. It pained Renee to think of her father behind bars from something she caused. Why hadn't she listened to Ram in the first place? Her family was going to hate her for what she'd done to Daddy.

Ramsey hugged Renee and Carmella as the officers released him. "I was afraid you'd be mad enough to do something this foolish if I told you what happened to Renee. I was only waiting long enough to hear from God about the right time to deliver such devastating news."

Ramsey pulled away from them. He pointed towards the door he'd just walked out of and then said, "I've never been behind bars before, but if it would get Renee out of the grips of that monster, I'd spend the rest of my life in there and wouldn't complain a bit."

"Hush with all that foolish talk. No husband of mine is going to prison."

"Yeah, Dad, Carmella already had to endure the shame of her ex-husband being sent to prison. How do you think she'd feel if she had visit you in here?"

"Let's just go home and pray," Carmella said.

Renee left the praying to her Dad and Carmella. She went upstairs and flung herself across the bed. The day had drained her of all strength. But every time she shut her eyes, she would see Marlin beating the life out of her. At about three in the morning when she could take no more of the melodrama in her head, she turned on the television and channel surfed.

As usual, nothing much was on TV. But she did come across an episode of Snapped. That particular show best fit her mood, so she turned it on. She had seen this episode before. It was about a bipolar mess of a woman who couldn't deal with the fact that her boyfriend no longer wanted to be abused by her. After harassing him for months, she'd finally driven to his job and shot him in the face right in front of his co-workers. The man had lived, but his face was a bit disfigured and his eye twitched as he spoke of the horrible ordeal.

Marlin had used, abused and caused her to lose her baby. Now he was taking pleasure in tormenting her and her family. She was so tired of being afraid of what lurked behind every corner... tired of living her life as a victim. But what could she do? Just like sin doesn't ask for permission, bullies don't ask if it's okay for them to ruin a life either.

***

"So the prototype of the new website has been built and you all are running off to the Bahamas to celebrate. I am completely jealous."

"Huh?" Jay turned to Tiffany and gave her a quick smile. She'd said something to him, but he had been lost in thought about Renee, wondering just how much abuse she suffered at the hands of a man who was supposed to love and protect her.

"You're distracted. You barely watched the movie and now you're not listening to me or eating your food. I know you've got a lot going on at work, but it's okay to relax now. You're at the finish line."

"My executives are still working."

"Your executives are getting reading to receive an all-expense-paid trip, they need to burn the midnight oil and with no complaints."

"I still feel a bit guilty about being out with you tonight. They have all put their lives on hold while I'm out for dinner and a movie."

"There's nothing to feel guilty about. You've cancelled every date we had scheduled in the last month. If you had cancelled on me tonight, I would have finally

She was tired of going through the same ole same ole with him. There had to be an end. "What do you want from me, Marlin?"

Calming down, Marlin began talking as if realization just struck. "You're never coming back to me, are you?"

"No," was all she said. She wasn't giving him reasons... wasn't trying to make him feel better about the rejection, just 'no'.

"So you don't want to help your father out of the jam he's gotten himself into?"

That wasn't fair. Of course she wanted to help her father. Closing her eyes, she bit the bullet. "What do I have to do?"

"Just meet me for breakfast. That's all I'm asking. If you do that, then I'll tell the judge that I provoked your father."

"And all I have to do is have breakfast with you?"

"Me and one of my business associates."

"I don't like where this is going, Marlin."

"No funny business. I just want you to have breakfast with us. As beautiful as you are, I will close the deal while he's staring at you."

Men had been using her as their little Barbie doll for as long as she could remember. But Marlin had been the worse. He seemed to think the only thing she was good for consisted of lying on her back or being eye candy. She hated him for suggesting such a thing, but she had to help her father. "Where do you want to meet?"

He told her and then Renee said, "I can't stay long, because I have to get to work on time."

As she headed toward the restaurant, Renee reminded herself that she had just agreed to meet with a man that she had a restraining order against. Even though she agreed to do this to help her father, Renee knew in her heart that her father would not want this. She pulled into a gas station and parked her car. She held onto the steering wheel as she remembered how Marlin held her on the floor and made her say that she was dumb and worthless. Sweat beaded across her forehead as she imagined such a thing happening to her again.

Marlin would be right about her being dumb if she allowed herself to get within fifty feet of him. She pulled her cell out of her bag, dialed her cell phone provider and asked them to change her phone number. She then threw the cell back into her purse and headed to work.

Turning on her radio, Renee tried to get the sound of Marlin's voice out of her head. Carmella said that praise music soothed her. Renee needed something to ease her troubled mind, so she turned to an inspirational station. Marvin Sapp was singing *Praise Him in Advance*. What struck Renee was the part of the song that said "Praise will confuse the enemy". She wondered if that was true and if it was, what was she supposed to do, just start shouting in front of Marlin. Maybe he would think that he'd finally driven her insane and leave her alone. Maybe all she had to do was just start playing with her lip or try to eat wax fruit.

She laughed at her silly thoughts. But as she pulled into the parking lot of her job, all her laughter dried up. Jay was standing outside talking with a police officer.

"What's going on?" she asked Jay as she approached.

He pointed to the back of the police car. Marlin was in the car with his hands cuffed.

Her hand flew to her mouth as she tried to figure out what must have happened in the space of time that she hung up with Marlin and drove in to work.

"I saw him sitting in his car when I came in this morning. I figured he was up to no good, so I called the police. They found a gun in his glove compartment."

"He came here to kill me?" Renee's eyes filled with fear. She didn't understand why he asked her to breakfast, if he planned to kill her at her job.

"Don't worry about it. I've got your back, Renee. Nothing is going to happen to you."

Jay reminded her so much of her brother, Ram. He'd thought he could handle everything that came his way, until the wrong thing came calling. Then the family had to call on God and all His angels to get Ram out of a jam he'd put himself in. She wouldn't allow Jay to get hurt trying to defend her. After showing the officers her restraining order, they hauled Marlin off to jail and then she told Jay, "I think it's best if I make today my last day here."

Jay took hold of her arm and went into the small conference room to the left of the front door. He pulled her close to him and wrapped his arms around her. When they pulled apart, Jay told her, "Looked like you needed a hug."

She did, but she hated that she needed it... and hated that Jay's hug felt so good and so right at a time in her life when everything else was so wrong. But she didn't trust her feelings or intuition anymore. If Jay felt good and right, then he had to be all wrong for her.

"Sit down, Renee."

She was shaking. Confusion swept over her. How could she have ever thought she was in love with a man as evil as Marlin?

"Calm down. Please let me talk to you."

"I've got to go. I don't want anyone here to get hurt because of what's going on in my life."

Jay put her hands in his, walked her over to the seat, and helped her sit in it. "That's what I want to talk to you about. Dean told me that he invited you on the retreat this weekend."

"He did, but I don't think I've contributed enough to be included on this celebratory trip." Renee hung her head. She was so tired of feeling inferior, so tired of being out of place.

"Dean never would have finished the program for Pro-Site 2 if you hadn't pulled things together for him. The man is a genius, but he can't find his way to the corner store without a GPS. Dean knows he owes the completion of this project to you. That's why he invited you."

"Are you sure?" Renee had a hard time accepting that she had actually added value to this project. After all, if it was true, she'd come a long way from the girl who could only prove her worth by lying on her back.

"Positive. And anyway, you could use an escape. So, why don't you take the day off, go home and pack your bags. Meet us at the airport tomorrow morning. I'll have Dawn get the info concerning your reservations from Dean."

"Okay Jay, if you think I've made enough of a contribution, then I'd love to go to the Bahamas this weekend." Renee left the office, feeling as if she had made the right decision. She needed to relax and forget about ex-boyfriends who were out to kill her. But telling her parents why she had left work early and that she would now be packing for the Bahamas, was more than she wanted to do with her day.

"I don't believe this," Ramsey exploded. He popped up out of his chair and paced the floor. "This is too much. Why is he even in Raleigh, anyway?"

"I guess he has some free time and decided to use it to harass me."

Carmella shook her head. "What's wrong with him? Why won't he just leave you alone?"

"He works for Satan, that's why."

"And you think running off to the Bahamas for the weekend is going to stop him?" Carmella asked.

"Maybe I should stay down there." She turned to her father. "Remember when you took us to the Caribbean when we were teens?"

Ramsey nodded.

"Remember that lady who stood on the corner with a fruit basket on her head. She charged people as they took pictures. Maybe I could earn a living doing something like that."

"That's crazy, Renee. Why would you want to do that?" Carmella asked.

"I don't. But I don't want to stay here, waiting on Marlin to make a move, either."

"Or maybe I should just go and buy a gun and then drive to Charlotte and sit outside his office building waiting on him."

"No Dad, I made the mistake of getting involved with Marlin and I will find a way to get out of this situation. But the last thing I want is for you to suffer because of my poor decisions."

***

"You are not bringing a gun in this house, Ramsey. How can you even think such a thing?" Carmella asked her husband with hands on her hips later that night, once they were in their bedroom.

"Something has to be done. I'm not just going to sit idly by and let that man kill my daughter." He then turned an accusing finger in her direction. "And while you and Renee were keeping secrets from me, Marlin could have killed Renee and I wouldn't have known anything about it."

"That's not fair, Ramsey. I didn't want to keep that from you. And I wouldn't have if Renee hadn't implemented steps to protect herself."

"Big whoop, you helped Renee get a restraining order that Marlin doesn't seem to care a thing about." Ramsey grabbed his pillow off the bed and then walked into the closet and grabbed a blanket.

When he came out of the closet, Carmella's eyes widened in shock. "What are you doing?"

"I'm sleeping downstairs, I can't sleep in here with you tonight."

She and Ramsey had been married for over a decade and in all that time, they had never slept apart. "Don't do this, Ramsey. Don't destroy what we have."

"I could say the same thing to you."

The look in his eyes told her that she had gone too far. She never should have agreed to keep Renee's secret.

She only prayed that their love would be able to weather this storm.

"You and I made promises to each other." He pointed from her chest to his. "I meant it when I said I'd never keep secrets from you. But now you've got me wondering what else you haven't told me."

"I made a mistake, Ramsey. I'm sorry about that. But I tried to get Renee to tell you what was going on. She was too ashamed. I kept praying..."

"Yeah well, we see where your prayers have gotten us." Ramsey shook his head as he exited their bedroom.

Lifting her hands as she looked heavenward, Carmella said, "What just happened, Lord?"

She got on her knees next to her bed with tears in her eyes. "My Lord, my God, Your word says that if I abide in You and You abide in me, I can ask what I will and it will be done. But I've been praying and praying about Renee's situation and things have only gotten worse. This man had a gun at Renee's job today. I trust You to take care of my family, Lord. I believe that You can bring Renee through this situation safely. I've witnessed You work on this family's behalf before. But I need You to step in so that my husband doesn't lose faith. Tears were streaming down her face as she ended the prayer with, "We are helpless without You, Lord. I don't know what to do, but turn to You. Please don't make us walk this road alone."

After praying to her Savior, Carmella was so fired up that she went into her office and turned on the computer. The devil was busy, but she wasn't going to let him destroy her family— not without a fight. And the way Carmella chose to fight was with praise.

She opened her email and began typing:

I will bless the Lord at all times: His praise shall continually be in my mouth. My soul shall boast in the Lord: the humble shall hear thereof, and be glad. O magnify the Lord with me and let us exalt His name together. Psalm 34: 1-3

Today has been one of those days where I would have rather just pulled the covers over my head and slept through all of it. But God is able to make all grace abound toward me and that is why I praise His holy name, no matter what is going on in the Marshall-Thomas household. Thank You, Lord Jesus for always looking out for my family... and this, too, shall pass. I believe it because I know my God.

She ended her email and hit send. Carmella had been vague about her situation on purpose. She wanted to give God praise, but she would never expose Ramsey to scrutiny, especially since the email went out to their seven grown children. For years now, Carmella had been sending out what she called praise alerts to her family. She needed them to understand that God is worthy to be praised, no matter what she or any one of them was going through—Praise Him Anyhow.

***

Far above the clouds, on streets paved with gold, Aaron, the captain of the host was passing out assignments to legions of angels. A group was being sent to help hurricane victims, another group was sent off to help with other catastrophes around the world. Then Captain Aaron called Arnoth to the front.

Arnoth stood like a soldier in the army of the Lord. "At your service, Captain, sir."

"Carmella Marshall-Thomas' prayers concerning Renee have shaken heaven and we have orders. It is time."

Arnoth was a warrior... a demon slayer for the kingdom. But perhaps a more accurate description of Arnoth's specialty would be that he aided the people of God in slaying the demons that held them in bondage. His new charge reminded him of Cynda Stephens, a woman who'd had her spirit crushed by every man she'd ever tried to love, until God sent that one man who would love away the hurt and anger that had taken root in her heart.

But the enemy hadn't been willing to let Cynda go without a fight. The battle had been fierce and by the time it was over, Cynda had given her heart to God and to a godly man by the name of Keith Hosea Williams. Arnoth had won the battle and had earned an extra jewel on his sword, but he'd come back to heaven with tattered wings. His wings had long since been healed, but even as Arnoth unsheathed his sword, he knew that he'd be coming back to heaven in need of another healing before he'd be able to begin the next battle. "We will fight, for all that is good and all that is right!"

Six

The Atlantis resort in the Bahamas was a sight to behold. There was something spectacular to do everywhere Renee turned. From the eleven pools, water slides, river rides, movie theaters and on and on it went. The place was decadent... definitely for the two percenters. A lowly assistant like her could never afford such a vacation. She could hardly believe that they were staying in the Royal Tower, the absolute best part of the resort, because the rooms were fabulous and the tower was centrally located near all of the resort attractions.

Dean had told her that she and Dawn would be sharing a room, so Renee was pleasantly surprised when they arrived at the reservation desk and discovered that they each had their own room. Their rooms were much smaller than the suites the executives had, but Renee didn't care. She was in the Bahamas, on Paradise Island, over seven hundred miles away from Marlin and she was going to enjoy every minute of her time away.

She had packed light, but she realized that no matter what Marlin was sending her through she didn't want to be so far away from her parents. And that whole idea about walking around with fruit on her head, was a non-starter.

"A couple of us are going to the beach. Do you want to hang out with us?" Dawn asked.

"Sounds good. Let me change into my bathing suit and get the novel I brought to read." Renee changed into her swimsuit and then grabbed her beach bag. She put her novel, a towel, small bottle of lotion and a sun visor in it. Then she rummaged through her purse for a few other items to put in her beach bag.

She grabbed her mints and a bottle of water. As she was pulling the Pure Life water out of her purse, Renee caught sight of the pepper spray she'd bought to protect herself from Marlin. She grabbed hold of it, getting ready to put it in her beach bag. But then she had this strange feeling, like someone whispering in her ear, telling her to put the pepper spray on the night stand next to her bed. She then grabbed her bag and left the room.

Down at the pool, Renee tried to concentrate on her book, but Jay was distracting her something fierce. She'd never imagined that he would look so good in swim trunks but his biceps, triceps and washboard abs were doing a number on her. She wanted to call Carmella and ask her to pray this lust demon away. She had been celibate ever since leaving Marlin, and Renee intended to stay that way until some man put a ring on her finger and waited for her to walk down the aisle and say 'I do'."

"Come on in." Jay splash water on her. "Put that book down and have some fun."

She didn't want to be anywhere near Jay. So she pointed at Dean who was stretched out on a lounge chair reading documents instead of frolicking in the pool. "He's reading, too."

"Yeah, but Dean has always been a fun snatcher. You don't want to end up like him." Jay got out of the pool and sauntered toward her.

Water dripped off of his body like he was making it rain. Renee was praying for a drought. She jumped off of the lounge, threw her book in her beach bag and said, "I've got to go back to my room."

"What's wrong with you?" Jay asked, as he watched her rush past him.

"I'll be back." She had to get away from Jay. As far as Renee was concerned if she liked Jay, there had to be something wrong with him. So she was going to stay as far away from him as possible. She had escaped from Marlin, and now she needed to escape from Jay. If things kept going like this, she might as well consider herself a runaway... maybe that was it, she was running away from false love that only sought to bring her harm. From this day forward, she wanted nothing to do with it.

Jason grabbed a towel and dried himself off. He then followed after Renee. When he caught up with her, he gently swung her around to face him. "Did I do something to upset you?"

She shook her head. "No, it's not about you. It's just... I just need to get away."

Smiling that gorgeous smile of his, Jay said, "We already did that." He did a sweeping motion with his hands, indicating the sand, the ocean and all the beauty before their eyes.

"What I'm trying to say is, I want to explore the island."

"Okay, then I'll go with you."

"No," she practically shouted in his face.

"I can't let you go off on your own, Renee. Your father would never forgive me if you turned up missing. We are not in North Carolina. You don't know this place like the back of your hand, so I think it's best if we travel together."

She wanted to argue, but deep down she knew he was right. It would be foolish to go off exploring alone. "Okay," she agreed, "but put some clothes on." She pointed at his nakedness as if it offended her.

Laughing, Jay said, "I doubt if the Bahamian women would want to hurt their eyes with such a punishing view of me. I'll get changed and meet you in the lobby."

As Jay rushed past her, Renee couldn't help but sneak another glance. She couldn't think of a single woman who wouldn't consider the athletically built, Jason Morris something lovely to behold indeed. She fanned herself as she channeled her stepmother. "I need to get my mind on Jesus."

When they met back up in the lobby, Renee was wearing a sundress and Jay had on a pair of tan shorts with a polo shirt. He grabbed her hand and said, "Come on, I know just the place."

Jay had a rental, so they hopped in the car and left the resort. Their first stop was Bay Street for some duty free shopping. But as she looked around at the high end jewelry, clothing and other merchandise, she told him, "Tax free or not, I can't afford this place."

"At least look at some of this stuff before you prejudge." Jay turned to the jeweler and asked, "Can I see that tennis bracelet?" He pointed to the one he was interested in and then pulled Renee closer.

The jeweler put the sparkling diamond and white gold bracelet on her arm, and Renee was captivated by the beauty of the thing. But then she thought about all the things Marlin had bought for her and the ways in which he had extracted payment and suddenly the bracelet wasn't so beautiful anymore. She took it off her arm and handed it back to the jeweler, and then told Jay, "I'm ready to go."

"What's your hurry, don't you like the bracelet?"

"Of course I like the bracelet, but it's three thousand dollars. I'm a lowly assistant, I don't have that kind of money."

"What if I wanted to buy it for you?" Jay asked, his eyes locked on hers, sending her messages she wasn't prepared to receive.

Folding her arms across her chest, Renee smirked as she told him, "It's still too expensive for me."

Blinking, he stepped back a bit. "What's that supposed to mean?"

"It means I'm not going to sleep with you just because you buy me a diamond bracelet."

"Whoa." Jay lifted his hands trying to pause the situation. "I'm guessing that Marlin dude must have really hurt you. And maybe a few other men as well, but that doesn't give you the right to assume that I'm just like them."

He stormed out of the jewelry shop and slammed the door to his car after getting in.

Renee gave the jeweler an apologetic half smile and then walked out, hoping that Jay hadn't been angry enough to leave her to find her way back to the Atlantis. But when she turned the corner and saw the rental car, she breathed easer. Jay had always been a gentlemen, even when they were in high school. Jay had always been the one to open doors for the girls and she'd never heard him say a disparaging word about the girls he dated... his jerk of a best friend had been the total opposite and had treated Renee horribly.

She arrived at the car; Jay leaned over and opened the passenger door for her. "Thanks."

He didn't respond, just started the car and drove.

"Where are we?" Renee asked after they'd been driving in silence a short distance and then parked.

"The Straw Market. A place where you can shop without needing to sell your body for the privilege."

She knew that she owed Jay an apology, but her pride wouldn't let her do it. Someone was always doing something to her, and nobody bothered to tell her how sorry they were. She opened the door and got out of the car and started walking around to see what this Straw Market had to offer. If Jay wanted to hold a grudge that was on him. She hadn't asked him to tag along, so he could either change his attitude or go on back to the hotel.

Renee spotted some cute little Bahama Mama t-shirts that had Joy's and Raven's names written all over them. Then she saw the "three for ten dollars" sign above the t-shirts and grabbed another one for Carmella. "Oh Jay, look at this," she picked up a straw hat that had Bahamas stitched on it and put it on his head. "I knew it would look awesome on you."

Looking in the mirror that was attached to the wall, Jay smiled as he slanted the hat. "I think you're right. I like it."

"Take it off. I'll buy it for you."

"Oh no," Jay shook a finger at her. "I'm not about to trade myself for a twelve dollar straw hat."

Jay had no idea what she had been through, so her accusation must have sounded hateful and mean spirited. She twisted her lip and then said, "I'm sorry. I shouldn't have said those things to you in the jewelry store."

Taking the hat off, Jay said, "But you did say them. And I'd like to know why."

"I was wrong. Let's just leave it at that, okay?" She turned away from him and took her t-shirts to the checkout counter.

"I don't want to leave it at that." Jay grabbed her arm after she handed the clerk ten dollars and then retrieved from the clerk the bag with her t-shirts inside. Jay ushered her out of the store saying, "I'd like to know how someone as beautiful and vibrant as you are could have ever fallen so low as to think you had to sleep with a man just because he offered to buy something pretty for you."

"I don't want to do this, Jay. I said I'm sorry, so let it go."

"What if I don't want to let it go?"

They were standing so close that she could feel the heat rising off of him as his nostrils flared. But he didn't have a right to be angry with her, so she snatched her arm away from him and said, "Then go back to the hotel and leave me alone."

Seven

Jay had better things to do than chase a woman who didn't want to be caught. He had never been spoken to the way Renee had spoken to him. Most of the women he dated appreciated the gifts he gave. But then again, he wasn't dating Renee and obviously never would. He simply needed to get those silly high school dreams out of his head. He was a grown man now, and if some troubled woman wanted nothing to do with him, well then, he was going to take the hint and move on.

They were having dinner beneath the stars at the Ocean Club. One of the premier dining spots on Paradise Island. Jay dressed in a Dolce & Gabbana white linen blazer and a pair of black slacks. It was stylish without being too formal. The room was elegantly decorated with a romantic candlelit fountain pool. However, Jay was all business as he shook hands and networked.

Then Renee walked into the room and knocked him off his game with that curves-for-days dress she was wearing. Looked like something the Duchess of Cambridge would wear to one of those fancy balls she attends with Prince William. Jay silently fumed as the men in the room fell over themselves as they rushed to get an audience with her. He doubted he'd be able to watch Renee prance around the room all night, so he clapped his hands, getting everyone's attention. "I'm sure you all have better things to do than hang around here all night. So, let's take our seats and order dinner."

Several members of their group shot questioning glances his way. One actually accused him of being the fun police, but he didn't care. Jay didn't owe any of them an explanation. As far as he was concerned they could just sit down, shut up, eat and leave him alone. He was the leader of this bunch, so he couldn't just go to the back of the room and ignore everyone, but that's what he wanted to do.

"Hey buddy, you want to tone it down? I'm getting questions about your mood," Dean told him as they sat down together at one of the round tables next to the candlelit fountain pool.

"What about my mood? Who said something about my mood?" Jay asked as if he was ready and willing to fire the culprit.

Dean leaned closer and whispered, "If you want her so bad, why don't you just tell her to come to your room tonight?"

"I don't know what you're talking about." Jay had never discussed his love life with Dean and he wasn't about to start tonight. Especially since the love going on between him and Renee was completely one sided.

Dean looked over his shoulder and then turned back to Jay. "All I'm saying is, Larry looks like he's about to make a move, so if you're interested, you better stop acting like a choir boy and get at her."

Jay turned to his business partner and blurted out, "She's not interested in me, okay? So just leave it alone." He closed his eyes trying to block out the pain those words caused him. Why had God allowed him to spend so many years dreaming about a woman who was off limits? And why had he been fool enough to convince her to take this trip?

"I'm sorry. I didn't mean to assume."

"Don't worry about it." Jay ate his food. Smiled and talked when appropriate, but as soon as dinner was over, he excused himself and went for a walk on the beach.

He needed to put as much distance between him and Renee as possible. After having time to think about it, Jay understood that offering to purchase a three thousand dollar bracelet for a woman he wasn't even dating was too extravagant. He wasn't upset about the refusal of the bracelet; it was the way she refused it that was sticking in his gut. She treated him as if he was some slime guy who preyed on women as soon as they got off the bus in a new city. Like he was going to wine and dine her and then put her on the stroll.

She was not the same Renee he'd pined over all those years ago. With a heavy heart, Jay accepted that fact and he also accepted the fact that it was time to stop dreaming and move forward with his life. He picked up a rock and threw it into the ocean. Tiffany had been after him to make a commitment, either they were in a relationship or they weren't. Jay had been prepared to tell her that they weren't. But maybe Tiffany was real and right for him. He threw another rock in the ocean and then lifted his head heavenward, praying for an answer. Since he was a child, his mother had taught him to trust in God. She'd run through the house shouting praises to a God that Jay couldn't see or touch. He hadn't understood her back then. But every time something good happened for their family... his dad got a promotion, Jay made the basketball team, they moved into a bigger house... his mother would tell him, "I prayed for that. Now I need to go thank and praise the Lord for bringing it to pass". So right now, Jay was praying for the Lord to do something for him. He'd received success and made tons of money. But Jay was still waiting on the one. "Can you please make it plain to me, Lord? Can you help me find the woman I will spend the rest of my life with?"

Steven stood between heaven and earth beckoning Jay to follow him.

The waters of the ocean shimmered and became this beautiful sight, as colors blended and stretched out as if a path to someplace was being set before his eyes. Jay was compelled to walk the beach, following the brilliant color. "Where you lead, I will follow," he said out loud hoping that God was listening.

***

"Come on, Renee, let's take a walk on the beach," Larry said as he took off his shoes and rolled up his pants.

She'd watched Jay walk away from their party and head down to the beach. He was in a foul mood and Renee had a feeling that she was responsible for it. She had apologized, so she didn't understand why he couldn't just accept her apology and be cool about it. Shaking her head, she told Larry, "You go ahead, I'm just going to sit here for a while."

"Suit yourself." Larry grabbed Dawn's arm and said, "Walk with me."

Dawn took off her heels and followed Larry and a few others down to the beach. Renee sat down on the steps that led to the beach. Jay had been good to her. He'd given her a job and looked out for her when Marlin came to her job acting a fool. Now she had offended him and that had not been her intent. She just didn't know how to relate to men anymore.

"Penny for your thoughts," Dean said as he sat down next to her with a drink in both hands. He held one out to her.

Renee stared at the drink, thinking of the time Marlin had slipped something in her drink and then she'd woken up in bed with one of his business associates. "No thank you. I gave up drinking about a year ago."

Smiling, Dean said, "More for me."

She smiled back at him and then said, "You seem a lot more relaxed this weekend. I'm glad the demo of the new site went over well."

"It did," Dean agreed, leaning back and taking a few sips of his drink. "Now Jay has to figure a way around his problems so we can get the IPO to go through."

"What's wrong? Why would Jay have a problem with the public offering if the new site is doing well?"

Finishing off his drink, Dean looked in her eyes and said, "You're beautiful, you know that?"

She'd heard those words more times than she cared to relive. There was always some man thinking she was beautiful and wanting to possess her so he could show her off and have his friends comment on her beauty. Marlin even went as far as sharing her with his friends. Beauty didn't mean a thing to her, not with the way she'd been made to feel on the inside.

"I don't think you need that second drink." Renee stood.

"Leaving so soon?"

"I'm going to turn in for the night. I have a book I want to finish."

"You're going to miss all the fun."

She smiled, but didn't respond to that as she headed back to her hotel room.

***

"Can't sleep?" Ramsey asked Carmella as she tossed and turned in bed.

She sat up, turned on the light and put her husband's hands in hers. He'd slept on the couch the night before, but was now, thankfully back where he belonged. "I'm worried about Renee."

"Renee is far away from Marlin, so she's fine."

Carmella shook her head. "Something has happened. I don't know what, but she's in trouble, Ramsey. We need to pray."

Ramsey jumped out of bed and reached for the telephone. "Let's call and see what's going on."

"No, let's pray first, then you can call."

Ramsey vacillated for about a second. He then put the phone down, climbed back in bed and held Carmella's hands. "Okay, I trust your discernment; let's pray."

***

Still feeling awful about how she treated Jay earlier, she put on her nightgown, sat down at the edge of her bed and pulled her cell phone out of her purse. There was only one message. Her dad was saying something about him and Carmella praying and that he wanted her to call home. But she had read Carmella's praise alert and knew that she was the cause of any discontent her stepmother was feeling.

Renee didn't know how to respond to that, especially since Carmella wanted everyone in the family to send out their own praise alerts. But Renee had nothing to praise God for. She sent them a text, letting them know that she was going to bed and would try to call in the morning. Hopefully by then she would know what to say to Carmella.

Grabbing her novel out of the bag, she stretched out on a lounge chair on the balcony and picked up reading where she'd left off. It would be an interesting diversion. Something to take her mind off of the friendship she had ruined. She read for about an hour and then her lids began to droop. The book was good, but she'd had an eventful day and it was time to shut it down. Walking back into her room, she turned off the lights, got in bed and then pulled the covers up as she drifted off to sleep and fell into a dream about Jay Morris' captivating smile.

He had that straw hat on his head again, but this time, Renee removed it from his head and purchased it for him. Instead of getting pressure from Jay about things she didn't want to talk about, they held hands as they walked down the street, back to his car. They reached the car and Jay opened the passenger door for her. Renee hesitated, then put her hand on Jay's face as she pulled him closer.

"What are you up to?" Jay asked as he inched closer.

Without answering, she got on her tiptoes and brought her lips to his with a hunger she'd never known before. The ravenous way in which Jay returned the kiss left her spent and in a state of undoing. Then just as they had come together, they broke apart. She could see him, but she couldn't get to him. No matter what she did, she couldn't get around the barrier separating them. Jay was her future, but she didn't know how to get to him.

"Calm down, baby, I'm here."

The voice penetrated her dreams and caused a chill to run up her spine as she felt the covers being pulled back and someone got in bed with her. Renee racked her brain, trying to figure out how someone could have come into her room. She'd not only locked her door, she'd latched it as well. But then she remembered that she'd been on the balcony reading her book and hadn't locked the sliding glass door when she'd come back into her room.

"I've come for what you owe me."

Her eyes widened. Had Marlin bonded out of jail and followed her to the Bahamas? But he didn't sound like Marlin. The man in her bed sounded like... she screamed as she hit the switch to turn the light on and then she jumped out of the bed.

"Where are you going? Don't you believe in paying your debts?"

"You're drunk, and I don't owe you anything."

"Either I'm going to get my night with you, or I'm going to get my money back." He reached up and grabbed her, pulling her back to the bed.

"Let me go. Leave me alone," Renee screamed, but it was no use. He wasn't listening.

Eight

Arnoth ran like the wind, his charge was in trouble and he needed to get someone to that room, quick, fast and right now. Jay was coming up the walkway; he'd spent the night at a church revival, listening to the anointed preacher, all the while praying that God would take the idea of Renee out of his heart.

Waving him forward, Arnoth yelled out to him, "Something is wrong with Renee. Hurry, I heard screams in her room."

Jay didn't even ask who the man was. As soon as he told him that Renee was in trouble, he sprinted into the hotel and told the desk clerk, "I need a keycard to open Renee Thomas's door. She's in distress."

"I'm sorry, sir, but I can't give you the keycard if your name isn't on the room reservation."

"Then you better follow me with that keycard, because I'm going to break the door down if I have to." Jay pressed the button for the elevator, but it was taking too long, so he took the stairs, three at a time. When he reached Renee's floor, he then roamed the hallway listening for sounds of distress. He called out, "Renee" every few seconds. He knew what floor Renee and Dawn were staying on, but that was it. In his haste to get to Renee, he forgot to ask for the room number. He wished the clerk would hurry up with that keycard. How could he help her if he couldn't find the room?

~~~

"Don't you touch me," Renee yelled at him as he attempted to run his hand down her back.

"That dress you wore tonight was beautiful. Did Marlin buy it for you?"

"You're a pig." Wrestling to get away, Renee managed to pull one arm free of his grip. That's when she remembered the pepper spray she had left on her nightstand. She leaned forward, reaching for it. She almost had it, but he pulled her back to him.

"Pig or not, you're going to give me what I came here for this time."

She dug her nails deep into his skin. As he yelped, releasing her to nurse the wound, she broke free and grabbed the pepper spray. When he tried to reach for her this time, Renee sprayed him, and kept on spraying until he held onto his eyes and screamed like he was being bludgeoned to death.

Her door burst open. Renee swung around, preparing to spray the newcomers with the spray. Although her attacker couldn't see, he kept coming after her, screaming, "You're going to pay for this!"

Renee stepped out of his reach as Jay rushed in with a hotel clerk right behind him, Renee dropped the spray and rushed into his arms. "Jay! I'm so sorry for what I said to you before. Thank you." She shivered in his arms as she said again, "Thank you so much for being here for me."

"Help me, Jay, I can't see."

Jay turned toward the man who'd called out to him, "Dean? What on earth are you doing in here?"

"He's drunk, Jay. He tried to rape me."

"Rape?" Dean said the words as if nothing could be further from the truth. "I was simply trying to get what's owed to me. Her boyfriend sold her to me and I never got the chance to collect until now."

Jay looked to Renee. "What is he talking about? Are you a prostitute?"

Without Jay saying another word, she knew his mind had just traveled back to this afternoon when she said she wasn't going to sleep with him for a bracelet. "It's not what you think. I have never sold myself."

"Do you want me to call the police, ma'am?" the clerk asked.

Completely mortified by the thought of anyone else finding out what Dean tried to do to her, she turned to Jay. "I don't want to talk to the police tonight. And if they believe Dean over me, I could wind up in prison on foreign soil." She was becoming hysterical at the thought of anyone believing that she was selling herself.

Jay handed a few large bills to the clerk and said, "Thanks for your help. I'll let you know if we need anything else." As the clerk nodded and left the room, Jay pointed to the door and said, "Get out of here, Dean."

"I can't go anywhere. She pepper sprayed me. I can barely see anything."

With a look of disgust on his face, Jay turned away from Dean. "Let's get your things, Renee. You're going to stay in my suite tonight."

Renee and Jay quickly grabbed her bags and headed out of the room. Once they were in his suite, he helped Renee to a seat on the sofa while he made her a cup of tea. Handing it to her, he said, "Drink this. It should calm your nerves."

Tears that hadn't come during the attack because she had been running on pure adrenaline, were flowing freely now. Jay sat down next to her and pulled her into his arms. "I'm so sorry that happened to you, Renee. Tell me what you want me to do and I'll get it done."

She wanted Dean to pay for what he'd done to her... wanted Marlin to pay, too. But that would mean that she would have to let the world know what a fool she had been. She kept trying to hide her secrets away in the corner of her mind, hoping they'd get lost and she'd never have to think about them again, but things kept popping up, causing her to relive the horrors of losing her baby, of loving a man whose motto for life was "you play, you pay". And she had paid dearly.

"Do you want to talk?"

She let go of Jay as she wiped the tears from her face. "Where do I start?"

He handed her some tissue. "Wherever you want. I'm here for you. And if all I can do to help is listen, then I'll do it."

"How 'bout we start with my first real boyfriend. Your best friend. The one who dumped me in college. But before he did, he told one of his friends on the football team that he could have me."

"The guy had asked me out on a date before Chris broke up with me, so of course I said 'No, I'm dating someone. I can't go out with you.' Chris laughed in my face and told me to guess who had given him my number."

"I never would have thought Chris would do something like that."

Shrugging, Renee said, "I guess I'm the kind of girl you don't just throw away... you give away, like a present or something."

"No," Jay said with force. "You're the woman that a man should cherish and look out for."

"I wish you had asked me out before Chris. I always assumed that you liked me. But when your best friend asked me out instead of you, I figured I had read the signs wrong or something."

Sorrow filled Jay's eyes as he lightly ran his hand through her hair. "You read the signs right. I was gearing up to ask you out, Chris knew it and he beat me to the punch."

"Things would have been so different for me if you had been my boyfriend in high school. Maybe we would have stayed together, huh? And then I never would have hooked up with Marlin."

There are a lot of woulda-shoulda-couldas in this world, Jay thought as he leaned his head against the back of the sofa without responding to Renee.

"You don't believe me, do you?"

"I don't want to badger you. Lord knows you've been through enough tonight. But I don't know what I believe, since you won't talk to me."

Turning her face away from his view, she said, "It's not that I don't want to talk to you. I've just been so ashamed of the things I've done."

Jay sat back up and put a hand on Renee's face, turning her back to face him. "The last time I checked, the only perfect person is Jesus Christ. So, this is a no-judgment zone. You can trust me, Renee. I look at you, and I wonder what happened to the bright, vibrant and confident teenager that I used to dream about. You've changed and I just want to know why?"

"But can you handle knowing?" Renee asked. She felt like a broken china doll. She would probably shatter into a thousand pieces if Jay turned away from her now.

He took her hands in his. "I won't let you down. You can trust me."

"I sure hope you're telling the truth." She gulped hard and then began. "First off, I want you to know that I am not, nor have I ever been a prostitute. But Marlin did things to me when we were together."

Hesitating for a moment, trying to hold onto her courage, she continued, "He once drugged me and then let one of his business associates sleep with me. He claimed that I cheated on him and just slept with a man I barely knew on my own. But I overheard a conversation where I discovered that this same man invested about a hundred thousand in Marlin's realty company."

"So he used you to get what he wanted out of this investor?"

She nodded. "With Marlin, everything is a commodity. She put her hand on her chin and added, "My brother told me that Marlin's business dealings were unscrupulous. But I didn't listen, because I was attracted to his good looks and his success. But the real estate market had dried up. He'd lost a couple of big deals and by the time we got together, even though I didn't know it, he was badly in need of cash."

"And where does Dean come into the picture? Why does he think you owe him?"

Renee shook her head. "I don't know. But I'm tired of talking about Marlin and Dean. I want to be free from the evil they have brought to my life." After a moment, it was as if she realized what that freedom would cost her and she said, "Oh my God. I have to quit my job."

Jay vehemently disagreed. He stood and began pacing the floor. "You don't have to quit your job. Dean attacked you. He's lucky you didn't call the police on him." Jay stopped pacing and turned to her. "Why didn't you call the police?"

"Nobody cares what some top level executive tried to do to me. I'm just his assistant. For all we know, the police would believe that I was actually trying to sell my body to him in order to move up in the company."

Jay sat back down next to her. "But you had me and the clerk to verify your claim. We saw what happened."

Lowering her head, Renee said, "You have your IPO to think about. What would have happened if the president of your company had been arrested this weekend for an attempted rape?"

"It wouldn't have been good for us. But I'm the CEO and majority holder of the company. I would have figured something out."

"It's not worth all of that. You've worked too hard to get where you are for someone like me to come along and spoil everything."

"Hey." Jay put a finger under her chin and lifted her face so that she was looking at him when he said, "You're worth so much more than you know."

She tried to smile, but it didn't quite make it across her face. "Thanks for saying that. It means a lot to me that you would think that."

"Why don't you believe it? That's what *I* want to know."

Tears welled in her eyes, as she realized that what he said was true. She didn't think much of herself. And hadn't for a long time. How else could she have loved a man who could beat a baby out of her?

"I'm sorry. I didn't mean to make you cry."

She waved his apology away. "It's okay. You're right. I don't think much of myself. I keep making all the wrong choices for my life. I'm just a mess." She stood up as she wiped the tears from her face. "Do you mind if I take a shower?"

"Sure. I put your things in the bedroom. I'm going to bunk out here on the sofa bed tonight."

"Thanks, Jay." Renee went into the bedroom, took a nightgown out of her suitcase and then went into the bathroom and jumped in the shower. But no matter how long she scrubbed, or how long she let the hot steamy water beat and batter her body, she still felt unclean. Jay told her that she was worth more than she knew. But it was so hard for her to climb out of this pit she'd dug for herself. So hard for her to imagine that there could be any worth in a woman who men thought nothing of passing around. So hard for her to believe that life could get better when everywhere she turned there was a reminder of her worthlessness.

Maybe everyone's life would be better if she wasn't around. Her father had been arrested and now had to deal with criminal charges for trying to defend her against Marlin. Now Jay was willing to throw his life's work away just to defend her honor. But she couldn't allow him to do that and she couldn't allow her family to suffer any longer.

As she got out of the shower, Renee came up with the perfect solution. Life was too hard for her and she was ready to admit defeat. She took the sleeping pills out of her purse and sat on the edge of her bed holding the bottle.

"You doing okay in there?" Jay asked from the other side of the door.

Renee put the pills back in her purse. "Just getting ready to lie down."

"Let me know if you need anything."

Jay had been good to her. Too good for her to kill herself in his hotel room. She decided that she wouldn't die tonight. But in the morning, Renee would tell Jay that she wanted to explore the island alone. Then she would take a few of her sleeping pills, walk into the ocean and never come back.

Nine

Jay rose early the next morning, after spending the midnight hours in prayer for Renee. She was hurting and he had no clue how to help her. But as he continued to pray, the Lord reminded him about the church he'd found. The ministry was having a revival that weekend and during the service he attended, they had read a brief bio of the woman who would be preaching this morning. He hadn't thought much about it as he left the church last night. But once everything had been revealed, Jay was now convinced that God had led him to that church so that he could take Renee to the service this morning.

He ordered room service and then jumped in the shower. Once the food arrived, Jay knocked on Renee's door. "Breakfast."

"I don't want any," she said groggily.

"Well, too bad," Jay said. "There's some place I want to take you this morning and I need you to eat first, because I don't know how long we will be there."

Renee threw on her housecoat and swung open the bedroom door. "I can't go anywhere with you today. I have plans."

"Have a seat." He pointed towards the dining room.

Renee didn't argue. She sat down and took the lid off of one of the plates. "A waffle with strawberries and blueberries?"

"I didn't know which one you preferred."

"Look at you, trying to make me feel all special."

She tried to smile, but Jay noticed that her lip only curved halfway and her eyes were void of laughter, as if she had died a little last night. But he was a firm believer in prayer. It worked; his mother had shown him that. Renee would be all right. "So, what do you have planned for the day?"

While cutting her waffle, Renee said, "I just want to explore the island a little more, that's all."

"Sounds like fun. We can do that—"

She cut him off. "No Jay, I want to go alone."

Don't argue with her, he coached himself. "I understand. Everyone needs a little time to themselves.

Matter of fact, I wanted to take you to this church that I found last night while I explored the area."

"I should have known. You always were a church boy."

"Hey, my mama raised me right. And if I do recall, you and your sister were in the youth group at church with me."

"Okay," she grinned, "I'll admit to having fun in the youth group."

"Then come with me this morning. I know you've got your own thing planned for the day. But do you think you could hang out with me for two hours this morning and then go do your exploring?" His eyes pleaded with her to say yes.

"How can I say no to a face like yours? Let me finish eating and then I'll get dressed."

***

Upon arriving at the church and seeing how the spirit of God was moving on everyone around her, Renee knew she'd made the right decision. Because Jay would be able to tell her parents that she had spent the morning of her death at church around so many people who were jumping, shouting and praising the Lord. When they finally pulled her lifeless body out of the ocean, Carmella would most probably say something like, "She's with God now." Renee smiled at the thought, because she knew that would bring comfort to her father.

This revival had all the bells and whistles of a Spirit filled revival. Fred Hammond and the United Tenors were on stage singing *Here in Our Praise*. Jay was rejoicing, feeling the love of the Savior that Fred Hammond was singing about, she guessed. But she wasn't feeling much love. Renee grew up in church just like Jay, but she still didn't understand how people were able to move past their problems and praise God like nothing else mattered.

After praise and worship, Renee tapped Jay on the shoulder. When he turned to her she said, "I'm not feeling this. I think I'm just going to leave."

"You came with me. We should leave together."

"I can catch a cab. It's not a big deal."

Then one of the ministers stood behind the podium and began reading the bio of the speaker. The minister said, "First Lady Cynda Williams and her husband, Pastor Keith Hosea Williams are no strangers to this ministry. They have prayed and supported us through the years. Pastor Keith preached at our church at least three times over the years. Today we are truly blessed, because we get to hear from First Lady Cynda this morning.

Jay whispered, "You can't just get up and walk out while they're introducing the speaker."

Renee admitted that it would be rude. She should have hightailed it out of there just before praise and worship ended. Now she would have to sit through the sermon.

"This warrior has been a soldier in the army of the Lord for many years," the minister continued, "but the thing most of you might not be aware of is that Cynda Williams wasn't always saved and sanctified, with a mind to run on for the Lord. Before coming to the Lord, she lived a life of drug addiction and prostitution. That's all I'm going to say. I'll let her exhort you with her testimony."

As Cynda took the podium, the congregation stood and clapped. "Take your seats, please." Cynda lifted her head toward heaven and prayed to God, asking Him to bless the congregation and to open their hearts to the message He called her to deliver from the foundation of the earth. "Turn with me in your bibles to Romans Chapter 8. She began reading in the first chapter:

There is therefore now no condemnation to them which are in Christ Jesus, who walk not after the flesh, but after the Spirit. For the law of the Spirit of life in Christ Jesus hath made me free from the law of sin and death.

For what the law could not do, in that it was weak through the flesh, God sending his own Son in the likeness of sinful flesh, and for sin, condemned sin in the flesh: That the righteousness of the law might be fulfilled in us, who walk not after the flesh, but after the Spirit.

Cynda closed the bible, looked out at the congregation and then said, "What does all that mean, you silently ask yourself. I don't know what it means for you, but for me it means that I don't have to condemn myself for the life I once led."

Renee was amazed that the beautiful woman standing behind the pulpit had once been on drugs and prostituted herself. She appeared so confident, so take charge. The more Cynda talked the more Renee soaked up.

Cynda was saying, "Before Christ came into my life, I had no discernment at all. Consequently, I ran after men who were all wrong for me. These men led me into a world of sin that I had no clue how to get out of. I eventually felt as if I didn't deserve any better than the life I was living.

"But then one day my husband came into my life and he showed me that I was worth far more than I gave myself credit for."

Hadn't Jay said the same thing to her? Renee glanced over at him. Jay was staring at her as if he was trying to see if she was hearing what the preacher was saying. She smiled at him and then turned back to the pulpit.

Cynda was now standing in front of the pulpit. She stretched out her arm and said, "I didn't believe that I was worthy of God's love. I didn't believe that I was worthy of anyone's love. But then one day, my Lord Jesus beckoned me to come to Him and ever since that day, I haven't looked back.

Standing behind the pulpit once again, Cynda glanced at her notes. "I know that some of you are wondering how I have been able to live my life without condemnation since I accepted Christ into my life... 'surely with the kind of life you led, there must be people who try to remind you of your past'." She looked out at the crowd, with good natured humor on her face. "See, I can read minds.

"And you're right. To this day, the evil one still tries to accuse me with my past. But whenever someone tries to get me down, I remind myself of those Bop Bags. You know the ones... they're inflatable and when you hit it, it swoops down and then pops right back up. You can't keep one of those Bop Bags down, and do you know why... because it's standing up on the inside."

Many of the congregants began to clap as if they got the message she was delivering. Then Cynda said, "And that's what we all need to do whenever Satan tries to bring guilt and condemnation into our lives, just keep standing up on the inside. Can I get you to do it now? Come on. Stand up for Jesus... stand up for the man or woman you are meant to be."

Without realizing what she was doing, Renee found herself clapping and pulling herself up from her seat. She had lived with condemnation long enough.

"And now I'm going to ask you to take another stand with me. If you want to know Jesus, the one and only person who can help you stand against the demonic forces that try to hold you bound, then come down the aisle right now... come and allow us to pray for you."

Renee hesitated, but only for a moment. She worried that if she went down that aisle, others would wonder why she identified so much with Cynda's story. But then she told herself to stand and let go of her foolish worries. She needed what was being freely offered to her.

She stepped into the aisle, making her way to Jesus, one of the choir members starting singing CeCe Winans' Alabaster Box. Renee stumbled as tears blinded her. For the first time in a long time, she knew without a doubt she had heard from God.

Cynda came down from the pulpit and pointed in Renee's direction. "It's you. God sent me here for you."

Renee was reminded of the movie The Help, when the maid told the little girl that no one seemed to want, "You is important and you is kind". God brought Cynda Williams all the way to the Bahamas just for her, because she was important to Him. "Oh thank You, Jesus," Renee said as she fell into Cynda's arms and allowed the woman to minister healing to her soul.

In the back of the room, invisible to human eyes, angels stood watching Renee transform from the caterpillar she once was, to the butterfly she would forever be, from now until eternity. They raised their swords and shouted, "Bless the Lord, for He is good!"

Then Arnoth commanded them to put their swords down. "We need to be vigilant, because I hear our adversary roaring like a lion. He isn't taking this one lying down."

"Well then, let the fight begin," Steven said, lifting his sword again.

***

"Oh my God, Jay. Thank you so much for bringing me to church this morning. I feel like God has given me a second chance. I'm born again, and all those terrible things that happened in my past didn't happen to me at all, but to the me I used to be." She twirled and danced as they made their way to his car.

"And just think, you almost left the church before the speaker delivered her message."

"Don't rub it in. I've been in a bad place for a really long time. I'm finally feeling good about myself, so don't try to bring me down."

"Okay Ms. Sunshine, get in the car; I'm taking you to lunch."

"Sure beats what I had planned for the afternoon." She hopped in the car; with the biggest grin on her face she said, "I'll even let you pay."

"Oh thanks for thinking of me. Let me see if I can find the nearest McDonald's.

Punching his arm, Renee said, "Hey, I just got saved, buster. Your old youth group buddy should deserve better than a burger and fries on a day like today."

"McDonald's has come up. They're serving chicken wings now."

"Whatever. I know you better not pull up at nothing with golden arches."

They continued their good-natured fun until Jay pulled up at Seafire Steakhouse. He killed the engine and then turned to Renee. They stared at each other, losing themselves in the sweet, sweet moment. Jay put her hand in his. "I need to tell you something."

"Still looking in his eyes, and feeling some kind of wonderful, she said, "What is it?"

"I have been in love with you since we were teenagers."

"What?" Her brows furrowed in confusion.

"You heard me."

"But you never said anything. You let me date that jerk friend of yours."

"Nobody told you to say yes to Chris. You could have waited for me to get my nerve up to ask you out."

Smiling at his comment, she said, "You were nervous? I can't believe that Jay Morris was scared of a girl. I mean, you dated just about all the cheerleaders."

"Only because I couldn't have you. None of the relationships lasted. And now I know why." He brought his hand to her face and gently stroked it. "You're the only woman for me. I want to spend the rest of my life loving you."

His hand felt warm and good on her face. His words penetrated her heart, but fear crept in and stole the moment. "Please don't do this now. I have to be honest with you. Love has never been something I've excelled at. And right now the only love I can trust is the one I found at church this morning."

"You can trust me."

Closing her eyes as a tear slid down her face, she said, "I want to trust you. I want to drop my defenses and love you, but I've been so wrong before."

Inching closer to her, he said, "You're not wrong about me."

Could she take a chance on love with Jay? He seemed like everything she'd ever wanted. But could she trust herself to make the right decision about the man in her life? She needed time... needed to pray. Renee shook her head; she was starting to think like her stepmother. What was the world coming to? She opened her mouth to tell Jay that she needed to pray about this, but before a word could escape her lips, he had captured her mouth.

The kiss was divine. It was magical and Renee didn't want it to end. But if she was ever going to have any hope of getting it right this time, she needed her wits about her when she prayed. So she moved away from the heat of his embrace. "We can't."

"Please don't push me away like this."

"Give me some time. I need to pray about this."

"I understand." But the look in his eyes didn't mesh with his words.

"I meant what I said last night." Renee touched his arm. "If I had dated you in high school, I believe my life would be so much different. But I'm tired of blaming other people for how things turned out for me. I have to take ownership. And that means I need to take a good long look at how I make decisions on who to connect myself with."

Nodding, he said, "Let's go eat." Jay got out of the car and then walked around to the passenger side and opened Renee's door.

"Why, thank you, sir; you are quite the gentlemen."

He held out his arm so she could wrap hers around it. Then they began crossing the street. Renee smiled at him, enjoying the fact that she was being treated in such a manner. Her radar had been way off before, but Renee had this one figured out. Jay was a good guy; she just needed to discover if he was the guy for her.

She wasn't left with much time to think about it, because the moment they stepped into the street, from out of nowhere, a car came barreling toward them. She tried to pull Jay out of the way. But once he saw the car, Jay pushed her out of the way and then he tried his best to get out of the way, but the car was coming too fast. Jay tripped, tried to get his bearings.

"Jay, watch out!"

Boom! The car connected and knocked Jay to the ground.

"No!" Renee screamed as she ran towards him. The car skidded as it sped down the street. When Renee reached Jay, she fell down on her knees next to him. His eyes were closed and he wasn't moving. She put his head on her lap. "Wake up, Jay. Please wake up."

Her eyes filled with tears as she looked around for somebody, anybody. "Help us! Somebody, please help!" she screamed while rocking uncontrollably. Jay wouldn't wake up. How could this be happening? "Don't you die on me."

Ten

"What color was the car?" Officer Daniel Scott asked.

"I don't remember... It was dark. Black, maybe hunter green," Renee said as she looked around as if she were lost and trying to figure out how she'd gotten to the spot she was standing in.

"Did you see the driver?"

"It all happened so fast. I barely saw anything. But I didn't need to; I know who did it."

"You have a name for me?"

She nodded. "His name is Dean Richards. He tried to rape me last night and then he tried to run me over, but Jay pushed me out of the way." Wiping the tears from her eyes with some tissue, she added, "I want to press charges." She wasn't worried about what others might find out about her anymore. She had given her life to Christ and she was standing up on the inside now. Nobody was going to do whatever they wanted to her and get away with it ever again.

"Where did this attack occur?"

"My hotel room. He came in through the balcony. I have two witnesses. Jay and the hotel clerk opened my door and caught Dean in the act of trying to rape me." Renee answered all of the officer's questions, and then the emergency room doors opened and Renee swung around. A nurse walked up to her; Renee asked, "How's he doing?"

"He's banged up. But we can't get him settled because he won't stop asking for you. Can you come back and let him see that you're okay?"

Turning toward Officer Scott, Renee said, "He needs me."

"Go on, I'll file the paperwork and bring it back for you to sign."

Renee followed closely behind the nurse, anxious to see Jay for herself. When they arrived at his room, Renee rushed in. "Oh my God, Jay. I was so worried."

He grimaced as he turned toward her. "I think my ribs are cracked."

"Quit moving around. Let me get the doctor," the nurse said as she left the room.

Smiling at Renee, Jay said, "Lady, I can't tell you how good it is to see your face. I must have passed out or something. Because I couldn't remember what happened to you."

"You pushed me out of the way."

"I did?"

She nodded. "If it wasn't for you, I'd be lying in the bed next door. You're such a good man, Jay Morris. I'm so thankful that you are in my life."

"You're just saying that because I'm all banged up," he joked.

She sat down in the chair next to his bed as the doctor came in to check him over. "Looks like you're going to be with us overnight," the doctor said.

Jay tried to object, but a pain shot through his body that caused him to bite down on his lower lip.

"We'll get you something for the pain, too."

"Can I get that pain medicine now?"

"It's on the way," the doctor said as he walked out of the room.

"I hate that you're in so much pain. I should be the one lying in that bed."

"Don't say things like that," Jay admonished her. "Even with the pain I'm in, I would be devastated if that car had hit you instead of me." The nurse brought the pain medicine in. Jay took it and then turned back to Renee. "What I'm wondering is why on earth that car came at us like that in the first place."

"I told the police that it was Dean. I also told them that I wanted to file charges against him for attacking me last night." She held her breath, not knowing how Jay would take the news that she had just put a monkey wrench in his IPO plans. She no longer cared what anyone might think of her, even if all the dirty details of her relationship with Marlin came out. But she needed Jay to be on her side.

"I'm glad you told the police about what Dean did to you. But I don't think he tried to run us down. He still needs me to finish this IPO."

Leaning back in her seat, she said, "Sometimes I wonder if Dean even cares if this IPO goes through or not."

"He likes money just like the rest of us; believe me, he cares." Jay's eyes fluttered as the pills began taking affect. "Don't go back to the hotel without me tonight. Ask the nurse to bring an extra bed or a reclining chair."

"If you don't think Dean tried to run us down, then why are you so worried about me going back to the hotel?"

"I don't know. But too much is going on. And I don't want anything to happen to you." He held out a hand to her. "I feel myself drifting off. Promise me that you'll stay with me tonight. I couldn't bear to lose you. I was so terrified when the police found that gun in Marlin's car. And now someone has tried to run us down. Just stay here, okay?"

"I promise. Now get some sleep. I won't go anywhere. Besides, I need to tell you about some files I found in Dean's office. But we can talk in the morning."

Within minutes, Jay was snoring and Renee was standing over him, watching while he slept. "Thank You, Lord. Thank You for keeping him alive."

Renee hadn't eaten a thing since breakfast. That car accident ruined their lunch plans and it was now after five in the evening. Renee found the cafeteria and purchased a sandwich and chips. On her way back up to Jay's room she ran into the policeman, Officer Scott.

"How is your friend?" he asked as he walked up to her.

"He's resting."

"Good. I brought the complaint for you to sign." They were standing off to the side of the hospital entrance.

Renee looked it over, then signed the document. Feeling good about finally doing something, rather than just letting awful things happen to her. "Thank you for taking care of this for me."

Officer Scott said, "If a crime happens in the Bahamas, we take care of it, don't ya worry."

As the hospital doors opened, Renee lifted her hand and pointed. "That's him."

"Who? Where?"

"Dean Richards. He just walked in." She pointed again. "He's standing at the information desk."

Officer Scott walked over to Dean and asked, "Are you Dean Richards?"

Dean turned to the officer. "Yes, I'm Dean Richards. Do you have news about my business partner?"

Officer Scott took out his handcuffs. "You'll need to come with me."

With confusion written on his face, Dean said, "What are you talking about? I can't go with you. I need to check on Jason."

"Ms. Thomas has filed a complaint against you for breaking into her hotel room and attacking her."

"You're not getting anywhere near Jay after you tried to kill us," Renee said as she got in Dean's face.

"Step back, ma'am. I'm taking care of this," the officer said as he put the cuffs on Dean.

"What is she talking about? I didn't do anything to them," Dean said as he was being ushered out of the hospital.

"I'm sure you didn't do it, just like you didn't sneak into my hotel room and attack me last night."

"You wanted me," Dean shouted back. You sell it for a living. And now you're lying to cover up the fact that you're a prostitute."

Renee was thankful that Dean had been taken into custody, but she was angry about what he'd said about her. She wanted to run up on him and scratch his eyes out, but then they'd both be going to jail. But she needed to get those words out of her head, so when she got back to Jay's room, she pulled out her iPhone, went to the app store and purchased the King James Version of the bible for her phone. She then pulled up an extra chair, propped her feet up and started reading. She needed something to calm the raging storm brewing inside of her. The word of God concerning condemnation had brought her peace earlier today. She decided to search the scriptures to discover who she was, so she didn't have to listen to the words running through her head... words meant to hurt her and bring doubt.

She stayed up late soaking in bible verses that told her she was more than a conqueror through Christ and scriptures that reminded her that though the righteous may fall, the Lord was able to deliver. By morning Dean's words didn't have the power to hurt or affect her self-worth. She was a child of the King, and that was all that mattered.

The doctor came in the room, looked Jay over and then said, "I'll be putting in your release papers, so you should be able to leave in a couple of hours."

"Thanks doctor, I don't feel like I've been run over by a train this morning, so that's progress, right?"

When the doctor left, Renee told him, "I'm going to head back to the hotel and get you a change of clothes."

"I don't want you going near that hotel without me."

"It's okay. Dean came to the hospital last night and the police arrested him."

"You had him arrested?" Jay sat up a little too fast and then grimaced from the pain. "I wish you had talked to me before doing that."

"I'm worth more than I know... remember when you said that to me?"

Jay ran his hand over his face. "Okay, you're right. You should have called the police the other night. I'll stand with you on this."

"Are you sure you're with me on this? Because if you need to get behind Dean so that your IPO will go over smoothly, I'll understand."

"I said I'm with you," he snapped. "You may not believe it, but you're worth more to me than ten thousand IPOs."

Smiling, she said, "Okay then, I'll go get your clothes and be back here within the hour."

"Hurry back."

Jay's car was still parked across the street from the steak restaurant he tried to take her to yesterday, so she took a cab back to the hotel. Most of the Pro-Site staff were packed and waiting on the shuttle to take them to the airport when she walked into the hotel.

"Oh thank God," Dawn said when she saw Renee. "We hadn't been able to find you, Jay or Dean. I was beginning to think that someone had kidnapped all of y'all."

"No kidnapping, but Jay is in the hospital. He got hit by a car yesterday."

"Why didn't you call us?"

"I'm sorry, Dawn, I should have called, but I wasn't thinking straight."

"What about Dean?" Larry asked as he came closer.

Renee didn't want to get into what happened with Dean in the lobby, so she said, "I saw him at the hospital last night. He's probably going to be staying behind a few days."

"Yeah, you're right. Dean wouldn't want to leave without Jay," Dawn said.

"Well, I'll see you all back in the states in a few days." Renee left them in the lobby and headed to the elevators. As the elevator made its way upward, Renee was once again assured that Dean had run over Jay. None of the others knew where she and Jay were, so the only way Dean would have known to look for them at the hospital was because he put them there.

Dean was such a creep that Renee was glad that she wouldn't be working for him anymore. She would miss the job, but it was time for her to start pursuing a career. What had all those years in college and all the money that had been spent on her education been for if not for her to spread her wings and soar? Her resume was getting updated the moment she returned home.

She opened the door to Jay's suite and went straight to his suitcase. As she opened it she was humming the lyrics to *Praise Is What I Do*. She caught herself and started laughing. When had she becoming a praiser?

"I don't think anything is funny. You kept me waiting here all night. I wonder how you're going to make that up to me?" she heard a voice say and then a chill went down her spine.

Eleven

"What time does Renee's plane get in today?" Carmella asked as Ramsey came into the kitchen.

"She's supposed to be here at about two this afternoon, but I haven't been able to get in touch with her." He sat down at the kitchen counter. "Did she call you?"

Carmella shook her head, put Ramsey's breakfast in front of him and then grabbed her cell phone. She dialed Renee's cell and when the phone immediately went to the voicemail, she waited for the beep and then said, "Hey honey, we were just calling to check on you. I hope you're enjoying your vacation. Your father and I just wanted to know if you need us to pick you up from the airport this afternoon." She hung up and then turned to Ramsey. "I don't feel right about this. I'm going upstairs to pray."

When Carmella went upstairs, Ramsey grabbed the phone and called Ram. As soon as his son answered the phone he said, "Have you heard from Renee?"

"Not in about a week or so. Why? What's going on?"

"I'm not sure. She went to the Bahamas with a group from her job, and we haven't been able to get a hold of her in the last two days. Carmella and I are getting worried."

"Is that what Mama Carmella's Praise Alert was about? Maxine and I've been praying for the two of you because we thought you'd gotten into some kind of argument or something."

"Thanks for praying for us, Son. I had been upset with Carmella over something that Renee told her, but I'm over it now." Ramsey then hung up with his Ram so he could call some of his other children. Raven's secretary informed him that she was in a conference meeting. His next call was to Ronny.

When he explained that he was looking for Renee because they hadn't heard from her, Ronny said, "That's not like Renee, she normally keeps in touch."

"That's why we're concerned."

"Did you call the hotel?"

"Last night," Ramsey confirmed. "They said she wasn't in her room. They couldn't reach her."

"There's something I need to tell you, Dad." Ronny took a deep breath and then said, "One of my business associates told me that Marlin made bail on Friday."

"Thanks for telling me, Son. I think I know what I need to do now." Ramsey hung up the phone and surrendered. He was big and strong and had handled most everything that came his way in life, including the untimely death of his first wife. But Renee was so far away that he couldn't get to her... couldn't help her if he wanted to. But he knew someone who could help his daughter better than he ever could. He opened the door to Carmella's throne room and said, "I think this is going to be *our* throne room from now on."

She was on bended knee in front of the makeshift altar she had constructed in the room. Holding out her hand to Ramsey she said, "Come, my love, the bible says that where two or three gather together in His name, He will be in the midst. God will bring Renee home to us."

***

Dropping the clothes she had been pulling out of Jay's suitcase, Renee stood and turned around to face her worst nightmare.

"Imagine my surprise when I discovered that you came all the way to the Bahamas to sleep with your boss, when you threw a drink in my face for asking you to do it to help me out," Marlin said as he inched toward Renee.

"I didn't sleep with Dean. You're insane."

"I'm not talking about Dean, nitwit. Jay is the one who was at my house that night."

"You're a liar!"

"How do you know?"

"Because I've known Jay since I was in high school. He's a gentlemen. He's nothing like you."

"Keep talking and I'll smack you in that stupid mouth of yours."

"You're right about one thing, I was stupid when I ignored my brother. I wish to God that I had listened to him and stayed away from you." If Marlin had come here to kill her, she was going to make sure that he knew exactly how she felt about him before he did.

He grabbed a handful of her hair and pushed her down on the ground. "Get down on your knees and tell me you love me," he said, mimicking an old movie.

But Renee wasn't intimidated by him. She shook her head. "I found love this weekend. So, I know what real love is and I could never feel that way about you."

Anger etched across Marlin's face as he slapped Renee across the face.

Her head fell back and then snapped back up like one of those bop bags Cynda Williams preached about. Renee smiled as she reminded herself to keep standing up on the inside. "Is that all you've got? My sister used to hit me harder than that when we were in grade school."

"How dare you talk to me like this?"

She stood back up and got in his face. "Get used to it. I'm not afraid of you anymore."

"So, you think being in love with Jay Morris will keep you safe from me?"

"I wasn't talking about Jay. I'm in love with my Lord and Savior, Jesus Christ. And His love is greater than all the evil you possess." As she said those words to him, Renee was silently praying, telling God that she wanted to live... wanted Him to rescue her from Marlin. But she also told God, "but if I am to be with You in Paradise, then that's all right, too. I just thank You for saving me".

Marlin reached behind him and when he brought his arm back around, he was holding a gun. "This is what I possess." He shook the gun in her face. "And if you keep talking, you're going to get one of these bullets between your eyes."

That didn't sound painless, so Renee shut her mouth. But she continued to silently pray.

"You don't have nothing to say now, do you? All that talk about Jesus has gone out the window now that you see what I'm working with." He waved the gun in the air. "Go on, call on Jesus. See if He can deliver you from my wrath."

When she didn't respond to his taunts he said, "Go on, call Him!"

"My God is able to deliver me. I do believe that," she told him.

"Then you're a bigger fool than I ever imagined." He walked over to her. Put the gun up to her temple and said, "Aren't you?"

"No."

"You got to the count of three to let me hear you say that you are a fool." He started counting...

Renee was not moved. She would never think less of herself than God had called her to think ever again. She would go to her grave knowing God's love and His peace, but she would never again say anything about herself that God hadn't said. "The word of God lets me know that I am fearfully and wonderfully made. I'm not a fool, I'm not stupid or worthless or any other name you can think to call me. I'm a child of God and that means something."

Sputtering from anger, he lifted the butt of the gun and slammed it down hard on her head.

***

"How many demons are in there with them?" Arnoth asked Steven.

"It's a room full of 'em and the more Renee talks about God the rowdier they are getting. We need to do something fast. I'm not sure how much longer she can stand against Marlin's assaults."

"We need to get Jay here so he can take care of Marlin while we go to war with his demons."

"I'm on it," Steven said as he disappeared.

***

Jay was leaning on the nurse button like an addict needing a fix. Something had happened to Renee. He had to get out of that hospital so he could go find her.

The nurse came in the room shaking her head. "Can you please get your finger off that buzzer? We already gave you your pain medicine and your breakfast."

"I want my release papers," Jay yelled at her.

"Just hold on. We're working on them. You'll be out of here soon enough," she said as she stormed out of his room.

Soon enough wasn't good enough for Jay. His ribs were all taped up, his back was still hurting, but he found the strength to pull the covers back and get out of that hospital bed. His clothes were folded on the chair next to his bed. The shirt he'd worn to church now had blood stains splattered on it. He put it on anyway, and then moaned and groaned as he bent down to put his pants on.

He caught his breath as he stood up and put his shoes on.

Steven stepped out of the room ahead of Jay with his sword. He felt the demonic forces approaching and he was ready to slay as many of them who dared to get in their way.

Twelve

"I have your sister," Marlin said as he held his cell phone to his ear.

"I want to speak to her," Ram said.

"And I want my money. I bet you'll be able to approve my loan now, won't you?"

"Let me speak to my sister!"

"Let's talk about my loan first."

"I had nothing to do with your loan being denied. It's not our fault that your credit profile is jacked. Stop borrowing money that you can't pay back."

Ignoring him, Marlin said, "Instead of the million I originally asked for, I now want five million. I want it wired to an account in the Bahamas, and I want it by end of business today."

"I'm not doing anything until I can speak with Renee."

Marlin put the phone to Renee's ear. She immediately said, "Don't give him anything Ram. Don't put your job in jeopardy."

"I can't just not do anything, Renee."

"Trust God. Tell Dad and Carmella that I went to church this weekend. I gave my life to the Lord, so I'm good. Do you hear me? I'm okay whatever way this turns out."

Marlin snatched the phone back and told Ram, "I have her tied up with a gun to her head. Does that sound okay to you?"

Ram sounded as if he was crying as he said, "No. Please don't hurt her."

"Get me my money."

"Okay, but even if I could somehow get the loan approved, we wouldn't be able to wire the money until tomorrow at the earliest."

"Then I guess you'd better work your magic." Marlin hung up the phone.

"Why can't you leave my family out of this? They have nothing to do with anything between us." Her hands and feet were tied to the bed post. But she didn't need her hands and feet to fight Marlin. Renee's weapon of choice was prayer and praise."

"What has gotten into you? I've never known you to be so aggressive. Do you really want this to be between you and me, because I don't think you can handle it?"

She didn't respond to him. Renee had something better in mind. Although she hadn't attended church much since going off to college, she had memorized the 23rd Psalm while in youth group. Back then, she couldn't imagine a situation where knowing the 23rd Psalm would come in handy, but she was sure glad she'd taken the challenge *"The Lord is my Shepherd; I shall not want. He makes me to lie down in green pastures: He leads me beside the still waters. He restores my soul: He leads me in the paths of righteousness for His name's sake. Yea, though I walk through the valley of the shadow of death, I will fear no evil: for Thou art with me."*

"Shut up!" Marlin screamed at her.

***

"Marlin has Renee, Dad. He just called and asked me to approve a five million dollar loan before he will let her go."

"Oh my God," Ramsey said as he sat down, looking as if life had dealt him a blow that he might not recover from."

"What's wrong? What happened? Carmella asked as she entered the family room.

Ramsey put the phone on speaker and asked Ram to repeat himself. Carmella sat down next to her husband

and Ram's voice was shaky as he recounted his conversation with Marlin.

"The blood of Jesus. Father, we need you," Carmella said.

"There's something else. Renee wanted me to tell you and Mama Carmella that she attended church yesterday and that she gave her life to the Lord. So, she said that she's okay."

Tears flowed down Carmella's cheeks as she turned to Ramsey and said, "Our prayers have been answered. God is with her, Ramsey, we don't have to worry."

"I believe that God is with her, but I still want my baby-girl back home. Can you go online and order our tickets to the Bahamas?" Ramsey said.

"Of course," she agreed with Ramsey and then told her stepson, "Ram, we need you to call your brothers and sister and tell them to pray like never before. Your father and I are going to the Bahamas to bring our child back. The devil can't have what God has blessed us with."

"I need to call and ask them for money. Because I can't approve a loan for Marlin that I know he's not going to pay. But I am going to close out my investments. That will give us two million."

"Your father and I have two million in our retirement. We can pull that out."

"Okay, I'll call Dontae. I'm sure he'll give us the last million," Ram said.

"Son, I want to thank you for your willingness to let go of your hard earned money for your sister."

"You don't have to thank me, Dad. I'd do anything for Renee, you know that."

***

Cynda and Keith had arrived home from their trip to the Bahamas. They were unpacking their clothes when Cynda turned to her husband and said, "Something is wrong."

"The kids are fine, hon. You told them they could stay an extra night at Isaac and Nina's house, remember?"

"I'm not talking about our children." She sat down on the edge of the bed. "Do you remember that girl I prayed for at church on Sunday?"

"The one that you believe God sent us to the Bahamas for?"

"Yes, she reminds me so much of me at her age. I was so insecure and broken after my mother died, that I allowed things to happen to me that no one should have to endure. When that young lady came down the aisle, God showed me the things she has suffered. She is free from all of it now, because she has allowed the precious blood of Jesus to wash her clean."

"But you're still feeling a burden for her?" Keith sat down next to his wife.

"I can't explain it, but I see her in a very dangerous battle that could cost her everything. I think we should pray for her and get a prayer chain started."

"Okay, you call Nina and ask her to get the prayer chain at their church going and I'll call the leader of our intercessory prayer team and ask her to get the chain going on our end."

After making the phone calls, Cynda and Keith came back together and got on their knees. Keith began the prayer, "Heavenly Father, thank You for Your grace and mercy. We praise You because of how You changed us and made us new. We praise You for doing the same for our dear sister, and we come to You now, asking for You to protect Renee. Send Your warrior angels on her behalf. Whatever seen or unseen danger that has tried to come near her, we ask that You send a way of escape for her."

***

"Why don't you just go on and shoot me?"

"How can you ask me something like that," Marlin protested. "Do you think I enjoy what I'm doing? I don't want to hurt you."

"That's laughable. They caught you at my job with a gun."

"It wasn't for you." He sat down on the bed and gently ran his hand along the side of her face. "You're beautiful. From the moment I saw you I had to make you mine. All I ever wanted was for us to be happy together. If you could forgive me, I'd gladly take you with me."

Did he think she was Boo-Boo the fool? Marlin had done nothing but torment her. Her life had become a nightmare. She'd even contemplated killing herself because of all that he had done to her. And he had the audacity to ask her for forgiveness. She'd sooner spit on his grave than give him such a thing. She knew full well that Christians were supposed to forgive, but she was new at this thing.

"You can't do it, can you?" Marlin stood back up, with the saddest look on his face she'd ever seen. "You lay there praying to God and quoting scriptures, but when I ask for forgiveness, you deny me."

She turned away, not able to face him. He had her tied up and still had the audacity to ask something of her. No, she wouldn't do it. He would be burning in hell before she even thought about forgiving him. "You did me so wrong. I fell in love with you and that meant nothing. You were ready to pass me around to anyone who asked, as if I was some toy to be traded."

"You were only too happy to spend my money when it was rolling in. Why shouldn't you help me when times got hard? You knew the real estate market had taken a nose dive. I was losing money right and left. I had to make a few deals." Marlin stared at her, trying to see if his words were sinking in. He then said, "It's not like I wanted to share you with another man. But I had no choice. Can't you see that it was the only way that we'd be able to continue our lifestyle?"

"I would have gladly returned everything you purchased for me, if I could just have my dignity back."

"You're such a cry baby." Marlin mimicked her, "*If I could just have my dignity back.*" Then he exploded. "What about my dignity. What about the fact that a man's self-worth comes from his earning potential and I was losing contracts right and left. But you don't care nothing about that do you?"

She looked him dead in the eye and said, "I care about the baby you beat to death. You killed my baby and you never even said I'm sorry. I could have forgiven you for the rest, but for that, I hate you."

"Isn't hate a sin?"

He'd struck a nerve with that one, because making it to heaven should be every Christian's dream, but hating Marlin might be the only sin that could possibly keep her from making it in. She prayed that she'd have enough time left on earth to find a way to forgive Marlin, because today certainly wasn't the day. "How can you dare talk to me about forgiveness after everything you've done? You're despicable and evil and I hate you. Dear God help me, but I hate him so much." Tears rolled down her face as the hate she felt seemed to wrap itself around her and refused to let go.

***

Long black tentacles massaged hate into Renee's brain. "That's right, remember everything he did to you. Remember everything that every man you trusted did to you. Don't ever stop hating Marlin. He did you wrong."

"Let her go," Arnoth said as he entered the room and took out his sword. He had been preparing himself for this battle and was determined that Renee would not lose the faith she had just declared because some demon wanted to fill her with hate... not on his watch.

"This is none of your business," the demon said.

"Oh, it's my business." He pointed to Renee and said, "She belongs to the Lord, and your demon hide belongs to me." Arnoth sliced through the tentacles that had wrapped around Renee's mind and then he took his sword and embedded it straight into the darkest part of the demon's being. It immediately disappeared.

One of the angels high-fived Arnoth. "Now that's how you slay a demon."

"Let's go to work," Arnoth said as the two angels dismissed all of the demons that had been egging the situation on. Now they only had one more to deal with. But he was big daddy of them all and he was hiding inside Marlin. They would have to find a way to get him out... and then they would slay him, too.

Thirteen

"Take me to the Atlantis, please," Jay said as he jumped inside a taxi cab. Steven rode on the hood as he watched for demonic forces that would try to stop them from getting to Renee on time.

The cabbie headed towards the Atlantis. About ten minutes into the drive, when they were just a few miles away, the tire blew out and the cab swerved. "What in the world...?" Jay said as he was swung from one side of the car to the other.

"The tire went out," the cabbie yelled back, as he expertly stopped the car and then got out and looked at his shredded tire. "I just bought that one. No way it should have blown out like that."

Holding onto his rib cage, Jay got out of the car and viewed the damage. "Do you have a spare?"

"Ya, man." The cabbie opened his trunk and took the tire out. He leaned the spare against the car and bent down on the ground, taking the shredded tire off. When he reached for the spare, it went rolling down the street like it was going fifty-five miles an hour.

"Aren't you going to go get it?" Jay asked.

The cabbie scratched his head. "You see how fast it left? I couldn't catch that tire if I tried."

Jay could see the Atlantis in the distance. He figured he'd be able to walk there before this cabbie got his act together. "How far on foot to the Atlantis."

"It's about a mile and a half away."

"I don't have time to wait for you to figure something out. I'm going to walk it."

"What about my fare?" the cabbie asked.

Pulling a ten out of his pocket, Jay handed it to the man and told him, "That's all you're getting. Next time make sure you're tires aren't rolling on worn out treads."

As Jay headed down the street, Steven was busy fighting off the demons that had attacked the cab. He had his hands full and was only thankful that the people of God were praying.

***

"What's taking so long with getting the answer on my money?" Marlin yelled into the phone.

"I'm working as fast as I can. I'll call you as soon as I know something."

"Your job isn't to know something... it's to make something happen, for your sister's sake."

"How is Renee?" Ram asked.

"She's getting on my last nerve. So, if you know what's good for you, you just might want to get me that money quick and fast." Marlin hung up and turned back to Renee. "Can you believe that? I don't think that brother of yours cares whether you live or die. I should have dated your sister. None of them would want her dead."

"None of them want me dead either. My family loves me."

"Yeah well, I can't tell."

"What happened to you? Why are you so evil?"

Marlin started strutting the room as if he was the king of the world. "Didn't nothing happen to me. Nobody is dumb enough to mess with me, because if they do, I always find a way to win."

"Like how you're getting back at my brother right now for beating you to a pulp? You could have gone to any bank for a loan. But you're doing this to get him fired, or worse. But I'm praying to God that your wicked plan for my family will not prevail. You don't have dominion over us. We belong to the Most High. He will take care of our light work." She looked him up and down with disgust written all over her face.

"I'm nobody's light work, baby. Believe that." He walked back over to the bed and squeezed her cheeks with his thumb and index finger. "Keep talking and I'll show you how much pain I can inflict on you." His hand traveled down the length of her body.

Renee squirmed, trying to get away from his prying hands. "Don't touch me. Don't you ever put your hands on me again."

"And what if I want to touch you all day long? You belong to me, I can do whatever I want to you."

"Untie me and I'll show you what I'll do about it."

Laughing in her face, he said, "I can hardly believe that you're the same girl who used to cower at the lifting of my hand."

She started to respond to that, but the door opened and Jay hollered her name. *Oh no, oh God, don't let this be happening.* "Run Jay, get out of here," she screamed.

"Where are you?" Jay asked as he searched the suite.

"Don't come back here. Run!"

"Looks like I'm killing two birds with one stone today. Tell me God isn't on my side," Marlin said as he picked up his gun and headed out of the bedroom.

"Thanks for joining the party. You saved me the trouble of going to the hospital to finish you off." Marlin raised his gun.

"Renee, are you okay?" Jay asked as he stared down the barrel of the gun that was trained on his chest.

"She's better than you are," Marlin said as he pulled the trigger.

The bullet lifted Jay off the ground and flung him against the back of the sofa.

Marlin ran back into the bedroom and untied Renee's legs and arms. "Come on, we've got to get out of here before someone calls the police."

"Where is he? Please let me see him." Renee was crying uncontrollably as they entered the living area of the suite and she saw Jay stretched out on the floor. "Oh God, no!" She pulled away from Marlin and ran to Jay's side.

Jay's eyes were fluttering. She put his head in her lap. "Don't die, Jay. Don't leave me."

"Y-you're okay," was all he was able to get out before his eyes closed.

"Nooo!" she screamed. "Why did you come after me? Why didn't you just wait at the hospital?"

"Get up. Let's go."

"I'm not going anywhere with you."

"I will put a bullet between his eyes if you don't get up and stop all that crying right now."

Renee believed that Marlin would do just what he said. She couldn't let him shoot Jay again, because she was still holding out hope that Jay could survive this blow. But if Marlin shot him again, then it would be over, and

Renee wouldn't be able to live with herself. She stood up and said, "Let me call an ambulance for him and I promise, I'll go with you, wherever you want to go."

"There's my obedient pup. But I'm not calling an ambulance."

"He'll die if you don't."

"That's exactly what I want him to do... die. Now come on." He grabbed her arm and pulled her out of the hotel room.

***

Carmella and Ramsey arrived at the hotel at two in the afternoon. They went straight to the police and informed them that their daughter had last been seen at the Atlantis and they had received a call from her kidnapper this morning.

Officer Corey asked, "Did the kidnapper tell you that he was calling from the Atlantis?"

"No," Ramsey said, "But Renee has a room there. We were hoping that you would be able to go out there with us and convince the hotel staff to help us search the hotel for our daughter."

"Thing don't work that way in the Bahamas. You can't just come here, claiming that we've got some kind of kidnapping scheme going on. The Bahamians are law abiding citizens. We're not interested in getting anything from Westerners but what they freely give."

Carmella jumped in. "I think you misunderstood. We are not accusing anyone here of kidnapping our daughter. We know the man who called, trying to extort money. He is a Westerner, and our daughter's ex-boyfriend."

"Ah, love gone bad, eh?"

"Very bad," Ramsey agreed.

Officer Corey appeared to be in thought, then he said, "Okay, I will help you. Let's get over to the Atlantis and rescue your daughter."

"Thank you, thank you so much," Carmella said as they followed the officer to his car.

"Don't thank me yet. We still don't know for sure that she is being held at the Atlantis." They got in Officer Corey's car and sped off.

Carmella put her hand in Ramsey's and said, "We're going to find her. God is with us on this journey; I can feel it."

Fourteen

"I know why you shot Jay. I know what you've done and I'm going to make sure you pay for everything you've done."

"Get in the elevator and shut up." Marlin pushed her forward as he put the gun in his jacket pocket.

"Where are you taking me?" she asked as the elevator descended.

He didn't respond to that question, but said, "If you draw attention to us when we walk through the lobby, I will shoot you on the spot. And wipe those tears."

She had to think of a way to get back to Jay, and she couldn't do that if she was dead. So, she wiped the tears from her face and stepped off the elevator as if this was just another ordinary day. Nothing to see here, the love of her life wasn't lying on the floor bleeding to death and she wasn't being held at gunpoint.

"Come on, let's walk down the beach, just like two love birds out for a stroll," he said as they left the hotel.

Jesus, I need You to show up for me. Lead me and guide me. Show me what to do, she silently prayed as they continued to walk down the beach. Then suddenly it came to her to sing praises to God, like she had been doing earlier. Things seemed to be getting worse the more she prayed and praised, but Renee was reminded of another childhood bible lesson they'd been taught about Joshua fighting the battle of Jericho. The wall didn't come tumbling down the first time the Israelites walked around the city, nor the second, third or fourth. It wasn't until the seventh lap that God caused the walls to crumble and allowed the Israelites to wage a victorious battle in Jericho.

So she started singing about Jesus and kept right on singing no matter how agitated Marlin became.

He grabbed her arm, and turned her around to face him. "Why do you have to irritate me?"

"Why do you have to be so evil?" With that question, a thought came to her mind. "Do you have to be so evil?" She looked in his eyes and saw pure darkness, but when she had been with him, she hadn't seen this kind of darkness in his eyes until it was too late. Now she understood what was going on. Stepping away from him, she shouted, "The blood of Jesus is against you... in Jesus' name I call you out now!"

***

"How dare you call me out!"

Slithering out of Marlin was one of the biggest, most elusive demons Arnoth had ever come in contact with. But he had put the words in Renee's mouth to get this demon to show his face, so now he would have to go to work. Failure wasn't an option, because it would cost Renee her life. "I'm over here, you gutless lizard. Come terrorize me," Arnoth goaded him.

The evil one slithered toward Arnoth. "Get a good look at her, Arnoth. This will be your last mission."

As Arnoth reached for his sword, tentacles stretched out and wrapped around him to the point of squeezing the life out him.

***

The clerk opened the door to Renee's hotel room. It was empty, but things were thrown around. "He must have taken her from this room," Officer Corey said.

Carmella bent down and picked up a small sprayer. She handed it to the officer. "This is Renee's pepper spray. I bought it for her myself." She leaned her head against Ramsey's chest, he rubbed her back for comfort as Carmella said, "Our baby is missing, Ramsey."

"And we are going to find her. Don't lose the faith on me now."

Pulling herself together, Carmella said, "You're right. We are bringing her back home." She turned to the clerk and said, "Her boss' name is Dean Richards. Can you call his room to see if he knows anything about Renee's disappearance?"

As they left Renee's room, the clerk called the front desk and asked a few questions. When she hung up she told them, "He's already checked out. There are only two people in that party who haven't checked out. One is your daughter and the other person is Jay Morris."

"Jay is a friend of Renee's. Can you call his room?" Ramsey asked.

The clerk contacted the front desk once again, the call was put through, but it just rang and rang. "He's not there."

Ramsey turned to Carmella, "Now what do we do?"

"I think we need to go to Jay's room. Renee and Jay could both be in that room and not be able to answer the phone." Turning back to the clerk she said, "Can you get us in Jay's room?"

The clerk looked at Officer Corey, "Are you requesting such a thing?"

Officer Corey nodded. "If we can get a look inside Mr. Morris' room, we could at least rule it out, if no one is in the room."

"Okay then, let's go get the key."

***

While Arnoth was taking the beating of his life from this enemy of the Lord, he tried to focus and figure a way out. Renee was depending on him and he couldn't let her down. He hadn't let down any of his charges throughout history and he wasn't about to start now.

"Let me go, Marlin. I don't want to be with you." Renee yanked away from him.

"You'll go once I get my money and not a second before. Keep walking."

"But Jay will die if I don't get back to him."

Grabbing her shoulders, Marlin pulled her so close that their faces were only inches apart. "Don't you ever say his name to me again. And since you're too stupid to get it, let me explain something to you. You wasted your love on a dead man." He shook her. Do you get it now? He was supposed to die."

She wasn't as stupid as Marlin thought. Renee had been putting things together and had planned to talk to Jay about it. Just to be sure, she asked, "So when you said that you didn't come to my job to kill me, you were telling the truth."

He nodded. "I told you. If you act right, I'll keep you with me. I just want the money that Ram owes me."

"He doesn't owe you anything. You're a thief and you always have been."

Marlin shoved and then slapped her.

The slap sent her reeling backward. She fell on her butt in the sand, but she was smiling wickedly. Because, just before he shoved her, Renee had slid Marlin's gun out of his pocket. She was pointing it at him.

"I guess you think you're going to shoot me?" Marlin asked, advancing on her.

***

"You will not torment Renee, not another day," Arnoth said as he took the demon by the throat and plunged his sword into the depths of him.

The demon sputtered and spat out venom as he decreased.

This one wasn't going easy; too bad for him that the saints of God were still praying for Renee. They hadn't given up and simply went about their business. So he pulled the sword out of the demon and plunged it back into the depths one more time. The second time did the trick. Instead of just diminishing inside, the demon vanished altogether.

One of Arnoth's wings had been slashed and tattered; he felt like passing out, but his charge was on the ground struggling with Marlin for the gun. He limped over to her.

***

"Let go of the gun, Renee."

"You let go," she said as they rolled around in the sand together.

As Marlin struggled to get the gun from her, he put his finger on the trigger and then turned the gun towards Renee. She felt herself losing control of the gun, but she wouldn't let it go. She wouldn't let him win like this. Then the gun went off.

***

"I could get in a lot of trouble for this if Mr. Morris is in there and doesn't want to be disturbed," the clerk said as they stood in front of Jay's door.

"And if he's in there gagged and tied up, needing our help, then what?" Officer Corey asked.

"Okay, I'll open it, but if I lose my job, I'm filing a complaint against you," she pointed a finger at the officer and then opened the door.

Ramsey rushed in. "Renee, Renee, are you in here?"

"Oh my God, Ramsey look," Carmella was pointing at Jay as he laid on the floor in a pool of blood."

Officer Corey went to check on Jay as Carmella and Ramsey searched the rest of the suite. As soon as they saw the ropes on the bed, they knew that Renee had been held hostage in this room. "Oh dear Lord, what has Marlin done?"

Fifteen

Marlin felt like dead weight on top of her. Renee pushed him off and then saw the blood oozing out of his chest. "Oh God, oh God!" Scared out of her wits, Renee scooted away from Marlin. His eyes were open, but they were void and distant. "I killed him."

People were walking or jogging along the beach, She turned to them. "Help! Help! I think he's dead... somebody, please help me."

Two men approached. One had his ear to his cell, talking to an emergency dispatcher. "Yes, a man has been shot... No, he looks dead."

The other man helped Renee to her feet. "What happened?"

"He kidnapped me. He had a gun, we tussled and the gun went off."

"The police will be here in a few minutes. Just wait here with us."

But that's when Renee thought about Jay. "I've got to get back to the hotel. He shot my friend. I have to check on him."

"The police will want to speak with you," the man with the cell phone said.

"My name is Renee Thomas; I'm staying at the Atlantis. And please, call the dispatch again, and ask them to send an ambulance to my hotel." Renee then took off running down the beach, back towards the hotel. She was determined that Jay was not going to die if she could do anything to help him.

As she ran, Renee felt as if she had jet propellers attached to her legs. She was running so fast that she feared she would fall on her face and then someone would have to come to *her* aid, rather than Jay's. But as she rounded the corner, see the ambulance. Renee wondered how on earth they got to the hotel so fast, but then again, she didn't care. She needed to direct them to Jay's room and get him to the hospital.

She approached waving and screaming. "Thank God... thank God you're here." But as she looked inside the ambulance she realized that the paramedics were not inside. "Where'd they go?"

Renee ran inside the hotel. She stopped one of the desk clerks and frantically asked, "Where are the medics? I need them to go to Jay Morris' suite. He's been shot."

"Ms. Thomas?" the woman asked, with wide curious eyes.

"Yes, I'm Renee." She pointed back towards the ambulance. "Where are the paramedics?" she asked again, hoping that she wasn't dealing with a language barrier.

"Mr. Morris is being brought down now. Your parents found him."

"My who?"

"Your parents… they came looking for you."

That simple statement from this woman reminded Renee of the bible story of the Shepherd who would leave ninety-nine sheep, to go look for the one that had somehow gotten lost. Her Dad and Carmella had always been a perfect representation of Christ to her. If it had not been for their guidance through the years, she would have never made it through this ordeal.

The elevator doors opened, Renee swung around to see Jay being wheeled down the corridor. "Jay!" she yelled as she rushed over to him. He was pale as a ghost. She grabbed his wrist and felt for a pulse. It was faint, but he had one. "Heal him, Lord, for my sake, please heal him."

"We need to get him to the hospital, ma'am. You'll have to let go."

Renee didn't hear the paramedic; she was too busy praying for Jay. But she felt herself being moved to the side as Jay was being lifted into the ambulance. "Let me go, please. I need to be with him."

"Don't worry, honey. We'll take you to the hospital," Ramsey said.

Renee swung around and fresh tears drifted down her face as she saw her father. She hugged him. "Thank you for coming after me, Daddy." She hugged Carmella and said, "Thank you, too, Mom. I'm so thankful that you're in my life." This was the first time she'd called Carmella "Mom" but it felt right. Like God had blessed her with a second chance at having a Mom to confide in and hang out with, and to treasure. She had all that in Carmella and she would never take her for granted again.

Carmella smiled. "Let's get you to the hospital."

"Not so fast," a detective said as he approached them. "I've got a dead body on the beach that needs to be accounted for."

***

It took a few hours, but after Renee relayed her story to the detectives and her family corroborated it, they let her go to the hospital to see about Jay. He had just come out of surgery and the doctor had high hopes for a complete recovery. Renee finally breathed easy.

She and her parents spent the night at the hospital, receiving periodic updates on Jay's condition. By morning he was woke and asked to see her.

Renee entered his room; tears were in her eyes as she stood over his bed looking at all the bandages and the tubes that were hooked up to him. Her man was alive, and she would forever praise the Lord for that.

"Don't cry. Except for busted ribs and the bullet they pulled out of me, I'm doing just fine."

"This is no time for jokes. I could have lost you yesterday. I don't know what I would have done if you had died."

"You would have survived."

Renee wiped the tears from her face. "I thank God that I'll never know." She leaned over and kissed him softly on the lips. "I love you, Jay, and I need you in my life."

"I love you, too, babe. I thank God for sending you back into my life... Now if I can just get you to stop hanging around dangerous characters, maybe I can date you without being run over or shot."

Sure enough, Marlin had been trying to kill Jay, but not for the reason he thought. "I wish I could take the blame for this, but I have something to tell you that you're not going to like."

"What do you mean?"

"All in good time, my love. Just rest for now. I've got a story to tell that will bring clarity to everything that has happened.

***

Jay stayed in the hospital for a week and a half. Renee refused to leave his side the entire time. So her parents decided that they would stay in the Bahamas for a second honeymoon. They all flew back to the states together and a week later, Jay called a private meeting with Dean.

"Everyone is so excited that you're back and can get to work on our IPO again," Dean said as he took a seat on the sofa in Jay's office.

"Everyone but you, right?" Jay asked as he joined his business partner and so-called friend.

"Of course I'm excited. We're going to be ten times richer than we are now. Why wouldn't I be thrilled about that?"

"Because of the dirty deals you made with Marlin Jones behind my back." Jay put a file on the table and opened it. "This document that Renee questioned you about clearly shows that you refinanced our building through Marlin's property development company. The two of you took two million in equity out of the building."

Jay pulled another paper out of the file. "And this document shows that we are not in default on that loan."

Dean held up his hands. "I can explain."

"Can you explain why you would try to have me murdered over this? Because that's something I'm very interested in."

"It wasn't my idea," Dean admitted. "When you got all excited about the IPO, I went to Marlin and told him that something had to be done about the money. He claimed that if I invested in his schemes I would get tenfold the return, but he had lost my money. So he figured that killing you would be easier than paying off a two million dollar debt."

"So much for friendship, huh?"

"It's not like that. I didn't want you dead. But I didn't have the money to fix the problem I created. I didn't want to go to jail."

"Speaking of jail. How did you weasel your way out of the rape charge against Renee?"

Dean put his hand to his face and rubbed back and forth. He then said, "Before your friend killed Marlin, he helped me grease a few palms and we fed them a story about Renee selling herself."

"Did you get all of that, Renee?" Jay yelled over his shoulder.

Stepping out of closet, Renee said, "I sure did."

Putting another document on the table, Jay handed Dean a pen. "As of this moment, I no longer have a business partner. If you sign this document, giving me ownership of all the programs you have created thus far, and relinquishing your percentage of the company, and then go quietly, then I will give you ten million. If you refuse, I will have you arrested. Your choice."

"Some choice," Dean said sullenly. He grabbed the pen and signed the document.

"Your things are being boxed up as we speak. I want you to leave this building immediately."

Dean opened his mouth to say something, thought better of it and just turned and left the building.

Renee sat down next to Jay. She put her hand in his. "I know that wasn't easy for you."

"Actually, it was fun."

"If you had so much fun, why did you give him so much money to go away? He doesn't deserve anything."

"If it wasn't for the public offering, I wouldn't have given him anything. But I can't afford a scandal at this point in the game."

Renee was so in love with this man. He was everything she'd ever desired. She didn't care about the money he was about to make. She would have loved him no matter what. Because, like God, Jay first loved her. She pulled him close, leaning into him, pressing her mouth to his as she kissed him with open abandon.

When they managed to pull themselves apart, Jay asked, "What are you doing for the next fifty years?"

"I don't know, why?"

"Because I want to marry you."

She shook her head. "If you can't promise me sixty years, it's a no go."

"Lady, I can promise you an eternity." He kissed her again and then said, "Make my dreams come true, Renee. Marry me and make me the richest man in the world."

She loved that his dream was no longer singularly about this IPO and becoming richer than Bill Gates. But it now included her and their love. She could work with that. "Yes Jay, I will marry you."

Epilogue

With her three-carat diamond ring on her finger, Renee sat down at her desk and opened her email. It was time to deliver the message her family had patiently waited for... it was time for her praise report.

Hey Family,

I know some of you probably never thought you'd see the day that I'd send out an email with the subject line of "Praise Alert". But I thank God that we serve a wonderful Savior who is able to make the impossible, possible.

I have been told how beautiful I am all my life, but I never felt beautiful. Not on the inside, where it counts. I think my problems with self-esteem began when I met my first bully in grade school. For a long time I pretended like I was okay and what that bully did to me hadn't harmed me. But it had... for so many years after that, I felt like I deserved no better than what I got out of life. Like I was nothing because that's what people kept telling me. But I thank and praise God because He didn't let it end that way. Giving my life to the Lord, has allowed me to lift my head and realize that I am somebody... I matter. I also praise God for the family I was born into and those my father merged us with through marriage. Because the love you all have for me is priceless.

"I never thought I'd be able to praise God while going through such horrific situations, but I did it. And now I, too, can say, praise Him anyhow!

Well, I'm off to make wedding plans...

***

Two angels stood outside the pearly gates of heaven shouting, "Glory to the Most High God!" They opened the gates and welcomed Arnoth and his soldiers back home.

It felt like déjà vu all over again as Arnoth limped in with tattered wings. He called out to his captain.

"Yes, Arnoth?"

"I have completed my mission."

"Well you have. I will talk to the General about your wings."

Bowing, Arnoth said, "Thank you, sir."

Captain Aaron disappeared from the heavenly hosts in the outer court. He walked through the inner court on his way to the Holy Place. There were unnumbered mansions in the inner court, room enough for everyone. Sadly enough, the beauty and splendor of heaven would only be enjoyed by the few that served God. As he passed by the room of tears, he glanced in and shook his head in wonderment. It still amazed him that humans had tears so precious that God would bottle and preserve them in a room as glorious as this.

He opened the door of the Holy Place and stood in the back, as he heard the voice of thunder and lightning. He then heard a multitude of praises. And as the voices became thunderous, Aaron also joined them. In this place, where God sits high and is lifted up, praises are sung to Him forever. His glory lovingly fills the atmosphere and joy spreads throughout His Heavenly court.

His omnipotence glistened through the emerald rainbow arched above the magnificent throne. The twenty-four elders surrounding Him, were also seated on thrones, and clothed in white radiant robes. They wore crowns of gold on their heads.

Seven lamps of fire were burning and a sea of crystal lay at the Master's feet. In the midst of the throne and around it, were four living creatures with eyes covering their entire bodies. The first living creature was like a lion, the second, a calf, the third, a man, and the fourth, a flying eagle. Each of the creatures had six wings. They did not rest day or night, as their massive wings enabled them to soar high above the thrones. Generating cool winds throughout heaven, they bellowed continuous alms to their King, crying, "Holy, holy, holy. Lord, God Almighty. Who was and is and is to come!"

The twenty-four elders fell down before Him and worshipped saying, "You are worthy, O Lord, to receive glory and honor and power; for You created all things, and by Your will they exist and were created." They threw their crowns before the throne in adoration.

Thunder and lightning sparkled from the throne of Grace once more, then Michael's glorious nine-foot form stood. His colorful wings glistened as they flapped in the air. "Yes, my Lord," he said, as he took the scrolls from the Omnipotent hand that held them.

Michael stood in front of Aaron. His sword was longer and heavier than the other angel's. Jewels were embedded throughout the handle of this massive sword, a symbol of his many victories. The belt that held his sword sparkled with the gold of heaven. "Here is your assignment."

Aaron took the scrolls, then said, "My General, my Prince, Arnoth has completed his mission."

Smiling, Michael said, "And so he has."

"Will he receive another jewel on his sword today, sir?"

"Let's get it done." They left the holy of holies and entered the inner court. The angels got excited at the sight of their general. After all these years he still amazed them. The one angel who could stand against Lucifer time and time again, and come out the victor.

Captain Aaron raised his right hand and the angels fell silent again. He passed out the assignments and sent several thousand angels on their way, then he said, "Arnoth, come forth."

As a sea of angels parted, Arnoth made his way to the front. He kept his head down, ashamed of the tattered condition of his wings. The wings that once flapped gloriously as he spread them were now torn, tattered and shredded. His beautiful white wings no longer flapped in the wind, they hung frail-like against his body.

"The battle was fierce," Michael said as Arnoth stood before him.

Arnoth's head was still bowed low as he wiped the sweat from his brow. His charge had survived the attacks of the enemy. He'd fought against legions of demons that tried to keep Renee bound. But those demons did not prevail. He told his general, "I'm just thankful that God still has some praying saints out there."

"Amen to that," Captain Aaron said.

Michael unsheathed his sword, and pronounced over Arnoth, "May the Lord strengthen you to do battle with the forces of darkness until the evil one is shackled." Then he touched both of Arnoth's wings with his sword, and they stretched forth as the wings on an airplane. And as his wings flapped in the air, they became glorious, with no sign of the ungodly battle he endured to bring one wayward soul back to God.

Don't forget to join my mailing list:
http://vanessamiller.com/events/join-mailing-list/
Join me on Facebook: https://www.facebook.com/groups/77899021863/
Join me on Twitter: https://www.twitter.com/vanessamiller01
Vie my info on Amazon: https://www.amazon.com/author/vanessamiller

Next book in the series
Praise For Christmas (Rel. Dec. 2013)
His Love Walk (Rel. Feb 2014)

Books in the Praise Him Anyhow series

Tears Fall at Night (Book 1 - Praise Him Anyhow Series)

Joy Comes in the Morning (Book 2 - Praise Him Anyhow Series)

A Forever Kind of Love (Book 3 - Praise Him Anyhow Series)

Ramsey's Praise (Book 4 - Praise Him Anyhow Series)

Escape to Love (Book 5 - Praise Him Anyhow Series)

Excerpt of FIRST Chapter of...

Tears Fall at Night

Book 1 in the
Praise Him Anyhow Series

by

Vanessa Miller

One

"I'm leaving you," Judge Nelson Marshall said, as he walked into the kitchen and stood next to the stainless steel prep table.

Taking a sweet potato soufflé out of her brand new Viking, dual-baking oven, Carmella was bobbing her head to Yolanda Adams's, "I Got the Victory", so she didn't hear Nelson walk into the kitchen.

He turned the music down and said, "Did you hear me, Carmella? I'm leaving."

Carmella put the soufflé on her prep table and turned toward Nelson. He was frowning, and she'd never known him to frown when she baked his favorite soufflé. Then she saw the suitcase in his hand and understood. Nelson hated to travel. His idea of the perfect vacation was staying home and renting movies for an entire week, but recently he had been attending one convention after another. And last week, he'd been in Chicago with her as she had to attend her brother's funeral.

Carmella was thankful that Nelson had taken vacation to attend the funeral with her, because she really didn't think she would have made it through that week without him. She and her younger brother had always been close, but after losing both their parents by the time they were in their thirties, the bond between them had become even stronger. Now she was trying to make sense of a world where forty-six-year-old men died of heart attacks.

Nelson had been fidgety the entire time they were in Chicago. She knew he hated being away from home, so she cut their trip short by a day. He hadn't told her he had another trip planned. "Not another one of those boring political conventions?"

He shook his head.

Nelson had almost lost his last bid for criminal court judge. Since then he had been obsessed with networking with government officials in hopes of getting appointed to a federal bench and bypassing elections altogether.

"Sit down, Carmella, we need to talk."

Carmella sat down on one of the stools in front of the kitchen island.

Nelson sat down next to Carmella. He lowered his head.

"Nelson, what's wrong?"

He didn't respond. But he had the same look on his face that he'd had the night they'd received the call about his grandmother's death.

"Please say something, honey. You're scaring me," Carmella said.

He lifted his head and attempted to look into his wife's eyes, but quickly turned away as he said, "This doesn't work for me anymore."

Confused, Carmella asked, "What's not working?"

"This marriage, Carmella. It's not what I want anymore."

"I don't understand, Nelson." She turned away from him and looked around her expansive kitchen. It had been redesigned a couple of years ago to ensure that she had everything she needed to throw the most lavish dinner parties that Raleigh, NC had ever seen. Nelson had told her that if he were ever going to get an appointment to a federal bench, he would need to network and throw fundraising campaigns for the senators and congressmen of North Carolina.

So she'd exchanged her kitchen table for a prep table, and installed the walk-in cooler to keep her salads and desserts at just the right temperature for serving. The Viking stove with its six burners and dual oven—one side convection and the other with an infrared broiler—had been her most expensive purchase. But the oven had been worth it. The infrared broiler helped her food to taste like restaurant-quality broiled food, and the convection side of the oven did amazing things with her pastries. She'd turned her home into a showplace in order to impress the guests who attended their legendary dinner parties. She had done everything Nelson had asked her to do, so Carmella couldn't understand why she was now in her kitchen listening to her husband say that he didn't want this anymore. "We've been happy, right?"

Nelson shook his head. "I haven't been happy with our marriage for a long time now."

"Then why didn't you say something? We could have gone to counseling or talked with Pastor Mitchell."

Nelson stood up. "It's too late for that. I've already filed for a divorce. All you need to do is sign the papers when you receive them, and then we can both move on with our lives."

Tears welled in Carmella's eyes as she realized that while she had been living in this house and sleeping in the same bed with Nelson, he had been seeing a divorce lawyer behind her back. "What about the kids, Nelson? What am I supposed to tell them?"

"Our children are grown, Carmella. You can't hide behind them anymore."

"What's that supposed to mean?" Carmella stood up, anger flashing in her eyes. "Dontae is only seventeen years old. He's still in high school and needs both his parents to help him make his transition into adulthood."

"I'm not leaving Dontae. He can come live with me if he wants."

"Oh, so now you want to take my son away from me, too? What's gotten into you, Nelson? When did you become so cruel?"

"I'm not trying to take Dontae away from you. I just know that raising a son can be difficult for a woman to do alone. So, I'm offering to take him with me."

"That's generous of you," Carmella said snidely. Then a thought struck her, and she asked, "Are you seeing someone? Is that it? Is this some midlife crisis that you're going through?"

"This is not about anyone else, Carmella. It's about the fact that we just don't work anymore."

Tears were flowing down her honey-colored cheeks. "But I still love you. I don't want a divorce."

"I don't have time to argue with you. Just sign the papers and let's get this over with."

She put her hands on her small hips and did the sista-sista neck roll, as her bob-styled hair swished from one side to the other. "We haven't argued in years. I have just gone with the flow and done whatever you wanted me to do. But on the day my husband packs his bags and asks me for a divorce, I think we should at least argue about that, don't you?"

He pointed at her and sneered as if her very presence offended him. "See, this is exactly why I waited so long to tell you. I knew you were going to act irrational."

"Irrational! Are you kidding me?" Carmella wanted to pull her hair out. The man standing in front of her was not her husband. He must have fallen, bumped his head and lost his fool mind. "What are we going to tell Joy and Dontae? I mean…you're not giving me anything to go on. We've been married twenty-five years and all of a sudden you just want out?"

"Like I said before, Joy and Dontae will be fine." He picked up his suitcase again and said, "I'm done discussing this. I'll be back to get the rest of my clothes. You should receive the divorce papers in a day or two. Just sign them and put them on the kitchen table." He headed toward the front door.

Following behind him, Carmella began screaming, "I'm not signing any divorce papers, so don't waste your time sending them here. And when you get off of whatever drug you're on, you'll be grateful that I didn't sign."

After opening the front door, Nelson turned to face his wife. With anger in his eyes, he said, "You better sign those papers or you'll regret it." He then stepped out of the house and slammed the door.

Carmella opened the door and ran after her husband. "Why are you doing this, Nelson? How am I supposed to pay the house note or our other bills if you leave me like this?"

"Get back in the house. You're making a scene."

"You spring this divorce on me without a second thought about my feelings, but you have the nerve to worry about the neighbors overhearing us?" Carmella shook her head in disgust. "I knew you were selfish, Nelson. But I never thought you were heartless."

He opened his car door and got in. "You're not going to make me feel guilty about this, Carmella. It's over between us. I want a divorce."

As Nelson backed out of the driveway, Carmella put her hands on her hips and shouted, "Well, you're not getting one!"

She stood barefoot, hands on hips, as Nelson turned what had seemed like an ordinary day into something awful and hideous. He backed out of the driveway—and out of her life—if what he said was to be believed. Carmella had been caught off guard...taken by surprise by this whole thing. Nelson had always been a family-values, family-first kind of man. He loved his children, and she'd thought he loved her as well. The family had attended church together and loved the Lord. But in the last year, Nelson had found one reason after another for not attending Sunday services.

"Are you okay?"

Carmella had been in a daze, watching Nelson drive out of her life; so she hadn't noticed that Cynthia Drake, their elderly next-door neighbor was outside doing her weekly gardening. Carmella wiped the tears from her face and turned toward the older woman.

"Is there anything I can do?" Cynthia asked, as she took off her gardening gloves.

"W-what just happened?" Carmella asked with confusion in her eyes.

"Come on," Cynthia said. She grabbed hold of Carmella's arm. "Let me get you back in the house."

"Why is everybody so obsessed with this house? It's empty, nobody in it but me. What am I supposed to do here alone?"

Cynthia guided Carmella back into the house and sat her down on the couch. "I'm going to get you something to drink." She disappeared into the kitchen and came back with a glass of iced tea and a can of Sunkist orange soda. "I didn't know which one you might want."

Carmella reached for the soda. "The iced tea is Nelson's. I don't drink it."

Cynthia sat down next to Carmella. She put her hand on Carmella's shoulder. "Do you want to talk?"

"Talk about what?" Carmella opened the Sunkist and took a sip. "I don't even know what's going on. I mean… I thought we were happy. I had no idea that

Nelson wanted a divorce, but evidently, he's been planning this for a while."

"You need to get a divorce lawyer," Cynthia said.

"I don't want a divorce. I don't know what has gotten into Nelson, but he'll be back."

"You and Nelson have been married a long time, so I hope you're right. It would be a shame for him to throw away his marriage after all these years."

Carmella put the Sunkist down, put her head in her hands and started crying. This was too much for her. Nelson was the father of her children. He was supposed to love her for the rest of her life. They had stood before God and vowed to be there for each other, through the good and the bad, until death. How could he do this to her?

"Here, hon. Dry your face." Cynthia handed Carmella some tissue. "Do you have any family members that I could call to have them come sit with you for a while?"

"My parents have been dead for years and my only brother died last week," she said miserably.

"Oh hon, I'm so sorry to hear that."

Carmella lifted her hands and then let them flap back into her lap. "I just don't understand. I thought we were happy."

Sitting down next to Carmella, Cynthia said, "I've been married three times, and honey, trust me when I tell you that you'll probably never understand. Men don't need a reason for the things they do."

They sat talking for a while, and Carmella was comforted by the wise old woman who had taken time out from her gardening to sit with her in her time of need. When Cynthia was ready to leave, Carmella felt as if she should do something for the kindly old woman. She ran to the kitchen and came back with the sweet potato soufflé that she had lovingly fixed for her husband. She handed it to Cynthia, and said, "Thank you. I don't know what I would have done if you hadn't helped me back into the house."

"Oh, sweetie, it was no problem. You don't have to give me anything."

"I want to. I made this sweet potato soufflé for my husband. But since he doesn't want it, it would bring me great joy knowing that another family enjoyed it."

"Well, then I'll take it."

After Carmella walked Cynthia out, she went to the upstairs bathroom. She lit her bathroom candles, turned on the hot water and then poured some peach scented bubble bath in the water. She got into the tub, hoping to soak her weary bones until the ache in her heart drifted away. The warm water normally soothed her and took her mind off the things that didn't get done that day or the things that didn't turn out just the way she'd planned. Carmella enjoyed the swept-away feeling she experienced when surrounded by bubbles and her vanilla-scented candles. But tonight, all she felt was dread. She wondered if anyone would care if she drifted off to sleep, slid down all the way into the water and drowned like Whitney Houston had done.

The thought was tempting, because Carmella didn't know if she wanted to live without her husband.

Tears rolled down her face as she realized that as much as she didn't want to live without Nelson, he was already living without her.

To finish the story, order your copy of...
Tears Fall at Night

About the Author

Vanessa Miller is a best-selling author, playwright, and motivational speaker. She started writing as a child, spending countless hours either reading or writing poetry, short stories, stage plays and novels. Vanessa's creative endeavors took on new meaning in1994 when she became a Christian. Since then, her writing has been centered on themes of redemption, often focusing on characters facing multi-dimensional struggles.

Vanessa's novels have received rave reviews, with several appearing on *Essence Magazine's* Bestseller's List. Miller's work has receiving numerous awards, including "Best Christian Fiction Mahogany Award" and the "Red Rose Award for Excellence in Christian Fiction." Miller graduated from Capital University with a degree in Organizational Communication. She is an ordained minister in her church, explaining, "God has called me to minister to readers and to help them rediscover their place with the Lord."

Vanessa has recently completed the For Your Love series for Kimani Romance and How Sweet the Sound for Abingdon Press, first book in a historical set in the Gospel era which releases March 2014. Vanessa is currently working on an ebook series of novellas in the Praise Him

Anyhow series. She is also working on the My Soul to Keep series for Whitaker House.

Vanessa Miller's website address is: www.vanessamiller.com But you can also stay in touch with Vanessa by joining her mailing list @ http://vanessamiller.com/events/join-mailing-list/ Vanessa can also be reached at these other sites as well:

Join me on Facebook: https://www.facebook.com/groups/77899021863/
Join me on Twitter: https://www.twitter.com/vanessamiller01
Vie my info on Amazon: https://www.amazon.com/author/vanessamiller

Made in the USA
Columbia, SC
25 March 2018